MIKE EVANS

The Year of Fifteen Summers

Stories from The Nine Fold Gate

Copyright © 2021 by Mike Evans

All rights reserved. No part of this publication may be reproduced, stored or transmitted in any form or by any means, electronic, mechanical, photocopying, recording, scanning, or otherwise without written permission from the publisher. It is illegal to copy this book, post it to a website, or distribute it by any other means without permission.

This novel is entirely a work of fiction. The names, characters and incidents portrayed in it are the work of the author's imagination. Any resemblance to actual persons, living or dead, events or localities is entirely coincidental.

Mike Evans asserts the moral right to be identified as the author of this work.

First edition

This book was professionally typeset on Reedsy. Find out more at reedsy.com

Contents

Foreword	iv
1 The Year of Fifteen Summers	1
2 The Nine Princes of Ophir	16
3 The Corpse Lay Deader	33
4 How Bera Reclaimed her Gift	64
About the Author	82
Also by Mike Evans	84

Foreword

Stories from the Nine Fold gate is a series of short tales of a dark, sometimes twisted, sometimes humorous, nature. They are set within the fantasy world of Ty-Gate, the location of the fantasy series *The Nine Fold Gate.*

Stories from the Nine Fold Gate is intended to be a standalone companion series to *The Nine Fold Gate,* which begins in 'The Scattered King' and continues in 'The Pursuit of Wolves' and 'The Eye of Chaos'.

You do not have to have read any of the previous books to enjoy this one.

During the writing of the books of *Nine Fold Gate,* I also wrote background stories. Mainly to give myself a better understanding of the cultures, characters, myths, and history of the world.

In this first volume you will find four stories.
   'The year of Fifteen Summers'
   'The Nine Princes of Ophir'
   'The Corpse Lay Deader'
   'How Bera Reclaimed Her Gift'

1

The Year of Fifteen Summers

There was a buzz in the air. A sense of anticipation and excitement that rarely attends meetings of the Senate. The rumour on the street had it that Crown Prince Hya-Dan Hassuy would speak.

Hya-Dan Hassuy was a bitter and bombastic man. A man for whom life was a series of tragic disappointments, caused mainly by his inability to see his own incompetence. But the people of Bassanai had loved his mother and so they loved him, and forgave his occasional foibles. I knew him better than most. I spent almost every evening in his company.

Of course, we all knew what he was going to speak about. The very same thing everyone had been talking about for the past one hundred and eighty months. I'd heard it from Hya-Dan Hassuy incessantly. I heard it in the streets, in the bath houses, and in the brothels. The courthouses were full of cases pleading special exemptions and the mortuaries were full of mummified corpses who couldn't be buried because they had not seen out the allotted time of waiting. In the temples and halls of mystery the people wailed and cried...

'When will this year end?'

It was a looooooong year.

In Bassanai, you see, a year is not dictated by the passage of the sun or by the number of moons or days that have passed. In Bassanai a year can only end when the prophecies ascribed to it in *The Great Book of the Years* have been fulfilled and the Hierophant of the temple of the book has turned green. This year there was one prophecy that had yet to come to pass and the Hierophant of the Book was still stubbornly blue.

Crown Prince Hya-Dan Hassuy was coming to speak in the Senate because he was upset. He had a lot to be upset about, to be fair. Tradition, law, and the will of the gods dictated that he must wait a full year from the date of the death of his mother, the Glorious Empress Hya-Thu Hummani, before he could rise to her imperial throne.

Well, Hya-Dan Hassuy had waited and waited...and waited some more. How he had waited! He had waited his youth away and still this interminable year showed no sign of ending. He had been in his prime when the empress had entered eternity. A strapping handsome man of forty years. Tall, well muscled, golden haired and beautiful. His eyes were said to be the most perfect blue ever seen and his prowess, in all areas, was legendary.

But now...well...his muscles had turned to jelly, his golden hair had thinned and turned lack-lustre and his prowess was drooped by wine. I had first hand experience of the latter as he was a regular patron in the Inn I owned with my wife. *'The Peacock and Ewer.'*

I myself had travelled to Bassanai at the behest of my own king, Tuderman of Channa, to attend the coronation and to present my masters fealty to the new emperor and offer him the gifts that had been sent with me. Nine peacocks, a cloak made from the fur of the bandergrumfh, and a magical golden jug of wine that never ran dry.

'Take these things to Bassanai,' He had commanded, as forcefully as he could for a worm of a man with a pronounced limp and a tendency to wink hopefully at every woman in uniform who passed him. 'They are for the exclusive use of the next Emperor, may they bring him succor in times of great need.'

Thank the gods for those gifts, that's all I can say. I could not leave, you see. Not until I had seen Hya-Dan Hassuy crowned and handed him his gifts.

Of course, my money had run out after three long months. But by then Ban-Thu Junna was pregnant and her mother had forced us into marriage. A happy accident, since Ban-Thu Junna owned an inn and I possessed a fertile flock of peacocks and a never ending source of the finest wine this side of the deserts of Ashay.

We had become quite wealthy.

I rather hoped Hya-Dan Hassuy would never be crowned. I did not relish having to explain to him that the roast peacock and ruby red wine I served every time he came into the inn, or the fabulously decadent bandergumfh fur he slept under when he had drunk so much that he could barely stagger up the stairs, were actually his all along.

So word on the street was that Hya-Dan Hassuy was coming to the senate to demand the closing of the year so that he might finally become emperor, and have access to the might and power that were dutifully his.

My own private view was that the Senate was unlikely to agree. They had become well used to administering the empire in that long year and, men being men, once they had a grip on power they would be unwilling to hand it over.

'Are you going?' Ban-Thu Junna asked me.

'Yes, I might.' I said. 'If I can get a place to stand in the citizens gallery.'

'Good.' She had said. 'On your way back, go to Floribunda's laundry. They have a bundle of sheets waiting for collection. You can save me the trek!'

That's one reason I married her, I suppose. She is a practical woman.

* * *

The citizens gallery was crowded. Far busier than I had ever seen it, but still I managed to find a position beneath the left buttock of the statue of Meura in her guise as the god of fishermen. By leaning on the pink granite tentacle of an octopus, I was able to peer down into the curia of the senate house. I found myself almost directly above the bald head of the Hierophant of the Book. She was an odd shaped woman built like one of those ancient figurines of the goddess of fertility; all hips and breasts with no neck and a tiny head. Her skin was as blue as sapphires, and her eyes as white as marble. The pages of The Book, you see, were soaked in magical ink and any one who touched it would be likewise contaminated.

She alone in all of Bassanai was allowed to touch the sacred text. Therefore she alone in all of Bassanai was blue, and she alone in all of Bassanai knew what the unfulfilled prophecy said.

She had a very tiny mouth. She didn't speak much.

Hya-Dan Hassuy entered, magnificent in golden robes and jewel encrusted crown, which by rights he shouldn't have been wearing. Can you blame him? To know that you are the rightful emperor but your word counts for nothing until a fat old woman turns green!

How frustrated he must have been!

Sadly, he didn't make much sense. He hadn't made much sense when I had spoken to him late the previous night either.

'I'm going, Possimus,' He had raged through wafts of wine scented breath. 'I'm going to do it. I'm going to make them tell me what 'waiting f..*hic*...or! Do you have more of that rather delicious wine? Beautiful stuff...and a touch more of that peacock? That would go down a treat...!'

He had sobered somewhat by the time he came to speak; had found time to return to the palace to change out of his vomit stained clothes. The one thing that had not changed was his anger. He was livid.

'According to the stupid traditions of this country my age is counted as 41 years!' he raged. 'In any other country, where universally twelve months comprise the passing of a year, not a month more, and not a month less, I would be 55. You have wasted me, sirs. Wasted me!

Fifteen years I have been kept waiting! For what? What is this unfulfilled prophecy that keeps our year from turning and our nation trapped? Tell me!'

'It is the will of the gods; we cannot change it' The Hierophant said in the shrill voice of a little girl.

'What does it say? What can possibly hold us in this nothingness of time?' Hya-Dan Hassuy screamed.

'The book is secret.' She said. 'I cannot tell you.'

'You will tell me!' Hya-Dan Hassuy was incandescent with rage now, fairly dancing on the spot. The flames burning in the little oil lamps that hung from the ceiling reflected off the gilded robe and sparked fires in the diamonds, and rubies, and emeralds of his crown. It was quite beautiful.

'I am your emperor, I demand you tell me!' He screamed. But the Hierophant of the book shook her little bald head.

'You are not.' Her voice was calm and flat but it kindled his rage to even greater heights. He fairly juddered with fury so that I could hear the jewels chattering together. His face went red, then blue, then a particularly uncomfortable shade of purple and little flecks of white spittle began to sputter from his lips and Hya-Dan Hassuy fell down in a heap on the floor; quite unconscious.

***

'She wouldn't tell me, Possimus!' Hya-Dan Hassuy whispered later that evening as he once again faced a platter of roast peacock and a jug of ruby red Ophirie claret. 'It's a disgrace. I ought to have her roasted like one of your birds...in fact...I will, once I am emperor. I will roast the lot of them and their damned book along with them!'

'Well, I for one am thankful.' Ban-Thu Junna said in that no nonsense style of hers as she put another peacock on the table. 'I am sorry for you, prince, but the longer you remain uncrowned, the longer we can remain in Bassanai. I have no desire to live in Channa. I hear it is a cold, miserable place.'

'The King of Channa who sent me is dead, Ban-Thu Junna. He cannot recall me.' I muttered, tersely.

'Channa? ' The prince asked, confused. 'Why would you move to Channa once I am crowned?'

Inside I winced. My wife has a mouth that runs without thought sometimes. She says what is on the tip of her tongue, and once it is said, there is no calling it back. She would start wars with that tongue were she in a position to do so.

'Because Possimus came from Channa to witness your crowning. Once you are crowned his own king will summon him home, most likely.' She said, neatly flipping the soiled cotton bib from beneath Hya-Dan Hassuy's chin and replacing it with a fresh one. 'He has only remained because he does not know from one day until the next if the prophecy will be fulfilled and you will be crowned!' Hya-Dan Hassuy fixed me with a penetrating gaze and I felt cold fingers of apprehension dance across my spine. I shot Ban-Thu Junna a look, one of the ones I reserved for the moments I was deeply upset with her. She didn't notice.

'You came from the King of Channa?' Hya-Dan Hassuy asked. I shrugged. What was there to say?

Hya-Dan Hassuy nodded, as if understanding.

'It is traditional for one king to send gifts to the coronation of another. And from that particular king I would expect great gifts. He knew my mother well!' he murmured. 'He must have sent you with gifts!'

It was certainly true that his mother had visited Channa in her later years. She had stayed a whole year. (A Channii year, not a Bassani year.) Indeed, there were rumours of a dalliance with some prince, perhaps even the King himself. Quite a scandal, given her age, but the stories spoke of a child born and hidden. There are always such rumours, people find romance in them. Being a child who never knew my parents I just find the sadness of cast off children.

'He...err...he...did.' I muttered. I must have gone red. As red as he had in the curia, but he just nodded again.

'And where are they?' He asked. Ban-Thu Junna had the decency to blush at that. She favoured me with a sorrowful gaze.

'Well, it's a secret that is better out than in.' She said, firmly. That's another thing about my Ban-Thu Junna, she can never say sorry, no matter how disastrous the mistake. And make no mistake this was a disaster.

And so I told the prince of the gifts the king of Channa had sent me with. Fortunately the crown prince laughed. He laughed long and hard, and when, finally he stopped laughing he waved a hand at me and said.

'Keep them, keep them. Had you given them to me when you arrived then I doubt I would have had as much joy from them as I have had eating each night at your table and drinking out of the fabulous magical ewer. And the nights I have slept beneath your roof have been more comfortable than the ones I have spent in my own bed, perhaps because of the beautiful bandergrumfh cloak I have slept beneath. '

I felt a wave of relief wash over me, and for a moment felt quite light headed; until he spoke again.

'But of course there is still a gift to be given.' He smiled. 'And I have thought of the perfect gift you can give to me.'

'Anything, my friend.' I blurted, happily. 'Anything at all!'

'Good.' Hya-Dan Hassuy grinned. 'I want you to break into the Temple of the Book and read the last prophecy of the year. The one that is yet to be fulfilled, and then come and tell me what it is. That way I can ensure that it is fulfilled and secure my coronation as emperor.!'

'Ohh...'Ban-Thu Junna said in a terribly small voice.

Myself, I said something a whole lot more rudimentary.

* * *

And so, the next night I found myself hiding in a closet in the antechamber of the Temple of the Book. It was midnight and an hour past the time that I had heard the great bronze doors slammed closed on the last of the pilgrims. I settled in my cupboard and listened as the business of the temple wound down and the slow measure of the night descended.

Ban-Thu Junna had given me a black light, and as I felt the temple fall silent about me I uncovered the light and exited my hidey hole.

This was not a large temple. The book after all is no God, and despite its status for the people of Bassanai it is not a thing that is worshiped.

Oh, people come and offer gifts to it, of course they do. Who doesn't want the prophecy of the coming year to promise increased wealth of health?

But I digress, as I say, the temple was not large. A small atrium led into a round, vaulted chamber. Doors to either side led to rooms and cells where the priests slept. One other door at the very back of the vaulted space led to a dark passage and the inner sanctum, where the book was housed.

I saw no one. The temple was strangely deserted. At the time I did not find that strange, so relieved was I that my trespassing was undetected. I should have known better.

Three quick paces and I was across the atrium and into the great round central chamber. A dozen more steps and the darkness of the passage to the inner sanctum closed about me and I took my first calm breath in what seemed an age.

There was a light coming from the sanctum. A cold, pale light that came from no flame. When I peeped inside I saw a granite pillar as high as my waist, and on it a great leather bound book.

My feet carried me to the pillar and I gently placed my hand upon the leather of the book. The cover was strange. Some form of leather, but made of tiny frills, like leaves all pressed together in a single sheet. It was from this that the glow emanated. I tried to recall all that I had been told about this book.

It was written, or so it was claimed, by a hermit who had lived in a cave high on the sacred mountain above the city. He had little to eat except lichen and snails. It was the snails which enabled him to see the future. They have a mild hallucinogenic effect, and can be quite intoxicating.

The book was closed but someone, I presumed the Hierophant, had thoughtfully placed a page divider approximately half way through. I flipped it open at the appropriate page, feeling a slight stinging tingle in my fingers as I did so.

The writing on the strange vellum was wavering and difficult to read. The ink was brown and faded and it took me a while to interpret the strange spider-like scrawl.

The she wolf brings forth two cubs,
  one born in sunlight, the other in shadow.
  One is older but the other wiser.
  One a drunk and one a soldier.
  One a King and one a fool.
  The book will tell you which to choose
  The book will tell you who will rule.

I pulled out a scrap of parchment Ban-Thu Junna had given me and an enchanted quill that never ran out of ink, and proceeded to copy the lines down as quickly as I could. Then I hurried back through the silent temple, back to my hidey hole in the closet. I would have to wait out the rest of the night in the tiny cramped space until the great bronze doors were opened in the hour before dawn. The streets were empty as I hurried home.

* * *

Ban-Thu Junna was waiting for me in the kitchen of the 'Peacock and Ewer'. As I burst through the door she turned to face me... and I saw the blood drain from her face.

'What is it?' I asked. I even looked quickly behind me to make sure that I had not been followed, but there was no one there. When I looked back at Ban-Thu Junna, her mouth was open and her eyes were as round as buttons.

'What?' I demanded as she sank heavily into a chair.

'You're green!' she whispered.

'Nonsense!' I snapped, rushing over to the press where we kept our best silver plates. I pulled one out and peered into its polished surface. My own tired face peered back. I had not slept well, pressed into a corner of a cupboard and alert to every step and creak of the temple. But, Ban-Thu Junna was right, I was green. As green as a pea. As green as a fresh leaf. As green as a parrot.

'Ban-Thu Junna!' I hissed. 'I'm *GREEN*!'

I have said my wife is marvelously practical, and she showed it then. Her shock lasted only moments before she was standing in front of me rubbing at my skin.

'It's not rubbing off.' she said. 'I will boil some water, you find the soap. The stuff I use to get unmentionable stains out of the sheets.' and she was off to fetch water from the well, and set a fire in the hearth.

Soap and hot water did nothing but make my skin hurt. Sand did even less. A salve of Beetroot, apple and pear just made me smell like a salad.

'We might conceal it beneath flour!' she mused. That just made me sneeze. Nothing would shift the emerald hue from my skin.

'Of course you know what this is,' she said, at last admitting defeat. 'The pages of the book. They are enchanted. That's why the Hierophant is blue.'

'But she is supposed to be the one who turns green.' I raged. 'Only when the last prophecy is fulfilled. Why have I turned green?'

'I don't know.' She shrugged. 'Maybe you reading the page fulfilled the prophecy. Maybe you messed up the magic; it's the sort of thing you would do!'

I was still green several hours later when Hya-Dan Hassuy arrived for his usual peacock lunch. He seemed more excited than usual.

'Today's the day!' he grinned at Ban-Thu Junna as he sat at his usual table. 'I saw them raising the flag to signal the ending of the year. Isn't that remarkable!'

'So she's turned green?' Ban-Thu Junna asked hopefully. Hya-Dan Hassuy shook his head.

'I suppose she must have, but I have no idea. Where is your husband, he must have a report for me, surely? This must be his doing!'

'Yes,' Ban-Thu Junna muttered, grimly. 'Yes, I think it probably is.' She sighed and waved me forward. I had been hiding in the doorway to the kitchen.

'Possimus...You're green!' Hya-Dan Hassuy laughed as he saw me. 'Well, that was always a risk, I suppose. So you touched the book then. Did you find the prophecy? What was it? Well done, by the way, you must have fulfilled it!'

Someone hammered on the door of the Inn. Ban-Thu Junna scowled.

'We're closed!' She screamed.

'Open in the name of the Emperor!' came a powerful voice.

'He's not here!' Ban-Thu Junna yelled back.

'Yes I am!' Hya-Dan Hassuy smiled, triumphantly. He pushed himself to his feet and smoothed down his robes, then saw a goblet of wine on the table. He picked it up and quickly tossed the contents down his throat, wiping away the ruby dribbles with a white silk sleeve.

'Open the door woman. Let my subjects in!' He demanded.

'Um...' I said, but no one listened. Ban-Thu Junna went to the doors and threw back the locking bar. In walked the Hierophant with her resolutely sapphire blue skin. In her tiny, pudgy hands she carried the glowing book. Behind her came a string of armoured generals.

'Well.' She said in the voice of a five year old; her white eyes seemed to stick me like arrows. 'By rights I should have you strung up and flayed. That's the penalty for touching my book, but right now I have questions.'

'The prophecy is fulfilled.' Hya-Dan Hassuy said. 'What questions can you possibly have? And why aren't you on your knees? You should all be on your knees. I am the emperor.'

The Hierophant sniffed, and pushed past him to drop the book onto the table.

'That,' she said, 'remains to be seen.' She flipped the book open to the required page, then licked her finger and quickly ran it across the words, muttering them under her breath as she did so.

'The she wolf brings blah, blah, blah...
One is older... but the other wiser.'

She looked at Hya-Dan Hassuy, then looked at me. In those

moments I think her eyes saw through my skin to my very bones. It felt most uncomfortable.

'You're definitely older, by at least a ten year.' she muttered to the crown prince. Her eyes flicked back to me. 'Wiser? Hmph...' Her finger slid further down the page.

'One a drunk and one a soldier.'

She looked back up at me. 'Please tell me you were a soldier!'

'I...was...' I muttered. 'In the army of Channa...I was a Captain of the Kings Guard!' She nodded, as if satisfied. Then glanced back at Hya-Dan Hassuy. 'I really don't need to ask you if you are a drunk, do I.' She asked.

'I!' he floundered. 'I'm the Emperor...' She was already moving on.

'This next line is most interesting.' She murmured. ' Because you clearly have no idea who you are.' she said to me.

'I am sent by the Late King of Channa to represent him at the coronation of Hya-Dan Hassuy, Crown Prince of Bassani.' I stammered. 'I would have been home years ago, but for that damnable book!'

'I would shut up, were I you.' she said. 'Lest you prove yourself to be the fool. An orphan of no account made Captain of the king's guard? A man of no birth sent to represent a client king to his liege Emperor. You are a bastard, sir. Born out of the right on both sides of the bed sheet and hidden from the world. Your mother could not bring you home, and your father had his own wife to keep sweet.'

My mouth flapped like a fish, but she was not finished. 'Now, it just so happens that your father was Tuderman of Channa, who died years past and left the throne to the sickly son of his only wife. Their only child.' She said. 'We received word this morning that the young King of Channa has died and left his throne to his half brother… Possimus the Bastard.' The Hierophant turned back to Hya-Dan Hassuy, an uncomfortable smile on her face.

'That makes him a King.' she said. 'What does it make you?'

'An Emperor?' He asked. The Hierophant shook her head.

'Not according to this.' She waved to the book. 'If only you had come yourself to read the book.' she sighed. 'Then you would be green, and you would be Emperor.'

'But…'Ban-Thu Junna stammered. 'Possimus can't be a king… he's…he's…Possimus!'

At least she still had faith in me!

'He is the bastard son of the king of Channa.' The Hierophant said. 'From his union with Hya-Thu Hummani, Empress of Bassanai. He is the rightful ruler of not one, but two realms.'

And then she was on her knees, and all the generals behind her were bending in their creaking clanking armour and they were all kneeling.

In front of me.

'But I'm the emperor…' the crown prince stammered.

'It seems not, brother.' I said, slapping him heartily on the back and handing him the silver ewer of never ending wine.

'It seems the year was only waiting for me!'

2

The Nine Princes of Ophir

In the far northern realms, where the snow and ice lay thick upon the land and the vast sprawling tundra is iron hard for most of the year, the tale I am about to tell is known as The Ninety Nine Princes of Ophir. In those frigid climes they brew a weak and piss poor ale and, in the depths of winter the sun breaks over the horizon for only three short hours. On those long bitter nights they have the time for such a tale, and few of them can drink so much as to fall into a drunken sleep. But here in the south, our nights are shorter and our beer stronger, so, for the sake of brevity, patience, respect for the aged queen Jusilla, I will discard the ninety.

Here then is the tale of **The Nine Princes of Ophir**

When Jusilla, wife of Hamma, King of Ophir gave birth to her first son, the kingdom of Ophir celebrated. It was a miracle. For Hamma and his wife were old, and had tried and failed many times to have children. Here, at last, was an heir; the future of the realm was secure.

He was strong and handsome, bright and golden haired. When

Hamma first held him, the babe clutched at the king's golden chain and no force or persuasion could make him let it go. How his father laughed.

'I have a strong son!' he cried in delight. 'The realm will be safe in his hands!'

There was, in all the joy of the moment, one small stain. A purple one that marred the boy's otherwise flawless complexion. A sinuous tentacle of wrongness that might almost have been a tattoo painted in the likeness of the arm of an octopus.

As Hamma was wrestling with his first born for possession of the royal chain of office, Jusilla coughed, and birthed a second son.

'Ohh!' she said.

'A spare!' Said the king.

'WAAAHHHH!' said the first son.

'Hic' said the second.

But this second son was not a spare. Indeed, had it not been for the fact that the second son was cradled in the arms of a nurse, and the first son was still gripping tight to the royal jewels; it would have been quite impossible to tell which was which.

They were as alike as peas in a pod and more alike than reflections in a mirror; even down to the sinuous tentacle of wrongness that marred their otherwise flawless complexions.

'Excellent!' Said the king.

'Cough!' said the Queen.

'WAAAHHHH!' said the third born son.

'Another?' Said the king. 'How delightful.'

'Cough!' Said the queen.'

'WAAAHHHH!' cried the fourth born son.

'Really, my dear, you can stop now!' said the king.

'Cough!' Said the queen.

Now, I am sure you are intelligent people. You know that this story is not called the five princes of Ophir. I could continue with the conversation as it happened. The king becoming increasingly distressed, the queen continually coughing and birthing sons until we get to the required number, but I think the point has been demonstrated.

I also think you can see why I chose to reduce the number of princes. That poor Jusilla...

At the end of the evening the king of Ophir sat beside his wife's bed cradling not one but nine identical sons. So alike that it was quite impossible to tell which was which.

They were all beautiful, all strong and all as fierce as lions. And all bore the very same sinuous tentacle of wrongness that marred their otherwise flawless complexions.

Well...there was one tiny difference. Hardly worth mentioning really. The very last one born, the ninth, was not a son at all.

It was a daughter.

'Are you quite done?' Hamma asked his wife in a slightly tetchy voice. 'What am I going to do with nine children?'

'Use your eyes, you foolish old man!' Jusilla said in an even more tetchy voice. And that is not to be wondered at considering the ordeal she had just been through.

'Look at the sinuous tentacles of wrongness that mar their otherwise flawless complexions.' She said. 'This is the work of the gods. They have blessed us!'

And she was right, of course. It was a blessing from the gods. Or rather it was a gift from just one god. Ty-shour, the tangled god who sits at the root of all things, whose sigil is...wait for it... the octopus.

Now, the astute among you will know all about Ty-Shour.

To the Gaesh he is the very last god you want looking in your direction. The dwarves call him the 'god of unluck' and in Bassanai he is feared more deeply than Aiasier, the lord of the sun and the vault of heaven, who dropped a star on the city of T'iu because they did not worship him loudly enough.

So, you may see that the blessing of Ty-Shour is not one to be celebrated.

You will be wondering what Hamma and his wife might have done to draw the eye of such a contrary and unwelcome god.

Well, if you are curious, listen on.

* * *

Our story now has occasion to slide widdershins to the path of time.

Not far.

Hardly a year, in fact.

Nine children.

Nine Gods.

Nine is a number to be respected.

To the very day, nine months before the birth of his children, Hamma was presiding over a conclave of his peers. Rival kings and queens from across the wide world, who had gathered for the dedication of a vast new temple to the nine .

Among the assembled crowns were Emperors, Empresses, Hierophants, Kings and Queens and all sorts of lofty types. It is a little known fact that when these people get together they can be just as catty, just as jealous, just as drunken and lecherous, rowdy, angry, maudlin, giggly, proud and arrogant as the poorest peasant or most obnoxious lordling. I know this to be true for I have traveled the courts of the world selling my stories and I have seen debaucheries that would make the madams in the cheapest brothels blush. So I at least am not surprised that soon an argument began between the king of Channa and Hamma.

Whose land was most blessed?

'MINE!' Cried the king of Channa. 'I grow the very best vines and my wines are like opium to the gods.'

'MINE!' Slurred Hamma, who had spent the last few hours sampling the Channian wine and liking it very much, thank you. 'My land is so beloved by Bera, the goddess of the wild, that she has filled my woods with the most majestic game in the world!'

'Well Channa,' Screamed the king of that land, 'has the best bees in the wide circle of the world. Our meadows are so filled with beautiful flowers, we make the very best honey you can find anywhere!'

'Channian honey is like gnats piss.' scoffed Hamma. 'Meura, goddess of the waters loves Ophir so much that she lives here for thirty weeks of every year. She fills our rivers and our lakes with the most delicious fish.'

And so the argument progressed. With each claim that the king of Channa made about his land, Hamma spoke of how the gods cherished Ophir more.

Aiasier, lord of the sky and the vault of heaven loved Ophir so much that he never gave a day too much sun, or a day too little, to ensure that all the crops ripened perfectly.

Velvet Schem, Goddess of the night and of the unseen, loved nothing more than to shine her silvery light on Ophir to heighten its beauty in the absence of her consort, the sun.

Even the four dead gods were brought into the argument. For though they were dead and cast beyond the nine fold gate into the neverafter, they still had opinions about the beauty and majesty of Ophir.

But drunk as he was, Hamma neglected to mention Ty-Shour.

Which was a bit of a shame. For Ty-Shour, the tangled god who sits at the root of all things, is also the god of the earth and the things hidden in it. And Ty-Shour had seeded Ophir with veins of purest silver and gold, beds of Sapphire and emerald and ruby, and rivers of iron.

This was the true wealth of Ophir.

And so, deep within his fortress which is in the very deepest deeps of the world where the light of Aiasier does not shine, Ty-Shour fumed and raged. And he plotted and he schemed ways to pay Hamma and Ophir back for their slight.

Now, Ty-Shour is called the Tangled God for a number of reasons. He resembles nothing more than a writhing mass of tentacles. He never walks a straight line when a twisted one is more interesting, and even the scholarrati who spend lifetimes trying to understand the gods find him impossible to fathom.

Ty-shour's revenge began that night when Hamma and Jusilla retired. The queen discovered that Channian red wine and Channian honey revived the rather limp ardor of her aged husband.

Nine months later Ham was born. And because he looked so much like his brother they chose to name the second child Ham as well.

I suspect Ty-Shour may have had a lighthearted tentacle in the naming of the children. For Hamma and Jusilla chose to name them Ham, Ham, Ham, Ham, Ham, Ham, Ham, Ham and Jane.

Madness, you may think. But they were so alike. And age just made them grow more alike, until absolutely no one, not Hamma or Jusilla or any of the Ham's could actually tell which was not the other ...or the other way around.

But Jane could.

Jane who was quiet and reserved and meek and compliant. Jane who watched her brothers grow and argue and fight over who was eldest, who would wear the crown, who would be general, who would be admiral, who high priest, who chancellor, blah, blah, blah...

And it was Jane who watched as they slowly realised that there were eight Ham's and only one crown.

Do you begin to see the first glimmerings of Ty-Shour's revenge?

* * *

As the children grew into young men, and Hamma and his wife just grew old, the people of Ophir began to ask who would be heir. Hamma and Jusilla despaired. Their sons spent all their time fighting and arguing about who was the eldest, the bravest, the strongest, the most intelligent and the most learned.

The problem for Hamma and Jusilla was that they really didn't know who was the eldest.

Hamma ordered a championship to be arranged where his sons could battle between themselves to be the bravest and the strongest and the most intelligent and most learned. The winner of each round would dip a finger into a pot of golden paint so that he would ever after be identifiable from his brothers. The winner of the tournament would be the son who had the most golden fingers.

This is actually the origin of the phrase *'He's got nothing left to gild!'* which means someone has tried everything they can, but still achieved nothing.

When the glorious day arrived the people of Ophir gathered

at the tournament field, all excited that at last their future king would be revealed.

Everything went well.

Ham won the wrestling contest and dipped his finger in the pot of golden paint.

Ham won the archery contest and dipped his finger into the pot of golden paint.

Ham won the running race and dipped his finger into the pot of golden paint, and so on throughout the day.

Then, just before the results were to be tallied, Jane, who had sat patiently watching her brothers contest, went to the steward who was charged with guarding the pot of golden paint and gave him a very large pot of spirit wine which she had drugged with a sleeping draught. She sat with him whilst he drank it down, and then she went to find her brothers.

When Hamma called for his sons to display their gilded fingers the entire tournament field held its breath…and eight Ham's held out sixteen golden hands and eighty golden fingers. The crowd groaned in dismay.

* * *

Another year passed. Jusilla died, and Hamma became even more old and bent than he had been. But still he had no notion of which Ham was eldest, bravest or any of the other things a King needs to be.

Jane came to see him one day.

'Father.' She said. 'Why not set a quest for my brothers. Something that will help you choose.'

'What quest?' Hamma asked. 'What could possibly help in this situation?'

'I don't know.' She sighed in that voice that girls use when they want their father to do something stupid for them. 'There's that dragon that's been eating people in the east vale...'

'You want me to send them to kill a dragon?'

'Well, it's been eating a lot of people.'

'But...it only eats shepherds really, maybe a few dozen sheep... now you want to feed it princes!'

'Now, father,' She said, twisting a lock of golden hair about one finger and peering up at him out of her flawlessly blue eyes. 'My brothers have been trained in every military art. Ham is an excellent bowman, and Ham can throw a spear over nine hundred feet, Ham is simply a beautiful marcher and Ham can do wonders with a horse in full panoply. Ham is strong enough to lift three elephants and Ham can climb anything. Let's not forget that Ham can charm bears out of the woods and Ham is a very, very fast runner. I'm sure they'll be fine!'

And so Hamma agreed. He summoned his sons and gave them the news.

'OOOH, great!' Said Ham. 'The dragon is toast!'

And indeed the dragon was toast. Ham sang sweetly to it and charmed it out of its lair. Ham threw a spear at it and pinned its tail to the ground and Ham shot it so full of arrows that people thought it was a giant hedgehog.

Unfortunately Ham, though a very fast runner, wasn't quite as fast as mega-super-hot flaming dragon breath and was burned to a crisp, and Ham, though a beautiful marcher was quite squished to goo when the dragon accidentally stepped on him.

On balance though the dragon slaying was a success. But it didn't really help Hamma.

'We need another quest!' Jane announced.

'Really, the last one didn't end so well.' Said Hamma.

'Something easy this time.' Said Jane.

'There's that plague of werewolves!' Suggested Hamma.

'Too dangerous.' Jane said after a moment's careful consideration. 'There is something I have been thinking of...but you'll hate the idea, I know you will.'

'Is it dangerous?' asked the king.

'Not as dangerous as a plague of werewolves.' Jane smiled.

'Then I'll probably love it. Tell me!' said the king.

'Well, in five days it's my birthday, and obviously the birthday of all six of my brothers as well. And every year you buy us all the same thing. Last year it was a helmet. The year before that it was a shield. Before that a battle stallion, before that a night in the local brothel, which to be fair was right up Ham's alley... but me...bit of a let down.

So, I was thinking, this year let's make it all about me. Your only daughter, the light of your life.'

'You didn't like the night in the brothel?'

'No, father. I spent it playing cribbage with a fat woman who wore only a basque and a powdered wig. On the plus side, it's a night I will never forget.'

'So tell me your idea.'

'Well, I heard a story last winter feast all about a horse that once belonged to Bera, the goddess of the wild. It's as big as an elephant and as green as new leaves in spring and as beautiful as meadow flowers in summer. It's name is Baltoothis.'

'You want Baltoothis?' asked the king, mildly appalled.

'That's the general idea. Yes.'

'*THE* Baltoothis, who eats human flesh! The Baltoothis Bera rode into battle against the city of Tantara, which had walls seventy feet high and fifty feet thick. '

Jane twiddled her hair and peered up at her father out of her big

25

blue eyes. 'I want him, father, and I will never ask for anything for myself ever again. Ever!'

'You do know Baltoothis toppled the walls of Tantara with one kick.'

'Oh, you know how these fables get exaggerated, father. I'm sure it wasn't like that really.' She smiled.

And so Hamma summoned his six sons and gave them the news.

'You must capture Baltoothis alive and unhurt.' Hamma instructed. 'This is, after all, a gift for your dear sister.'

'Easy!' Said Ham. 'I'll sing him a song that will make him gentle as a lamb.'

'I can climb into the trees and throw a net over him.' Said Ham.

'I'll throw spears in a cage about him that he cannot break out of.' Said Ham.

'I'll dress him in full panoply of gold and ride him to the palace.' Said Ham.

'I can lift him off the ground so that he can't use his formidable hooves!' Said Ham.

'If anyone like an elf shows up to rescue him, I will shoot it with my bow!' Said Ham.

And it was indeed easy...ish.

Ham sang a lovely song to Baltoothis and strode confidently up to the great horse with a smile on his face. Baltoothis snapped him up in one mouthful.

Ham dropped a net on Baltoothis and Ham threw a fence of spears about him. Ham crawled underneath Baltoothis and lifted him clear of the ground and Ham saddled Baltoothis with a solid gold saddle and with Ham carrying the horse, Ham rode him back to the palace.

Ham remained behind, shooting arrow after arrow at the hoards of angry elves who came to rescue Baltoothis. There were many more elves than there were arrows.

Ham was never heard of again.

'Daughter,' Said Hamma when his four sons had returned. 'Here is your gift. It proved more costly than I realised.'

'Thank you, father.' Jane cried. 'But he's a lot greener in this light than I thought he would be, and I have such pale skin. If I ride him I will just look ill. Let's just let him loose in the royal stud. Just think what magnificent battle stallions we will rear from his seed!'

* * *

'Father.' Said Jane one evening. 'May I show you something.'

'Of course.' said the king, and slipped his arm through Jane's as she led him out on to the terrace overlooking the deep port of Ophir. It was late and the sun had already dipped behind the rim of the world and the moon was high. Across the midnight blue waters, not three miles distant, they could see the lights of the port city of Gullesh, which belonged to the kingdom of Channa; their bitter enemy.

'Do you see the lights on the water, father?' Jane asked. 'They are Chanii ships. The Channii are massing a great fleet. They intend to invade. If only we could stop them. But our own fleet is old and worm ridden and I fear the Channii will crush us in a fair fight.'

'I fear you may be right, girl.' Sighed Hamma. 'But what can we do?'

'Well, funny you should say that, but I've been thinking. ' Said Jane. 'It occurs to me that my four brothers are all excellent swimmers.More than capable of a short swim of three miles, or maybe six if they swim back. It also occurs to me that Ham is exceedingly strong, and as all of my brothers are identical in all regards, then the other three must be exceedingly strong too.'

'As always your logic is flawless.' Said the king. 'Is this going to get any of them killed?'

'No.' She said. Then, as if realising what he had said...

'NO.'

and then

'Oh, father, no. Nothing so grim.'

'So what's your idea?'

'If my brothers were to swim out to the Channii fleet and each of them were to take say ten ropes with strong hooks attached, they could each hook ten of the ships and then swim back to Ophir, towing the ships behind them. Then we, not Channa would have an immense fleet of war ships and we could then invade Channa and bring them under your majestic rule. You would be king of both Ophir and Channa. A kingdom vaster than any other. Equal in size to the Empire of Ahsay...in fact, father, now that I think of it...it would *BE* an Empire, and you would be an Emperor.'

'Oooh, I rather like the sound of that.' Hamma said.

And so everything that Jane had suggested was put into motion and the Ham's were sent to swim across the strait to Gullesh where they each hooked ten of the Chanii war galleys to their ropes, and then began to swim home.

It nearly worked.

Except for the sharks.

Lots of hungry sharks.

Ham, who was strong enough to lift three elephants, got eaten first. Then Ham, who was exceptionally good at throwing spears.

Finally it was Ham, who could climb anything, who found that there really wasn't anywhere to climb that was out of the reach of sharks.

Ham, who could do wonders with a horse in full panoply, jumped on the back of a shark and rode it back to Ophir pulling not only his ten ships, but the thirty ships that his brothers had been towing.

So that was good.

Hamma quickly raised crews for his forty new ships and filled them with his cavalry, all mounted on great green stallions descended from Baltoothis, and he launched an invasion of Channa. Within days it was all over. The Channii surrendered after their king got eaten by the Ophir cavalry.

Hamma was crowned Emperor.

But Hamma still had to choose an heir. And he had only one son left. Ham, who could do wonders with a horse in full panoply. And so, given no option, Hamma named Ham his heir. How the people of Ophir celebrated....for a while...because as soon as he had named Ham heir, Hamma dropped dead.

Jane, though. What about Jane? Well; Jane was, of course, bitterly disappointed. But it is also true to say that she was not surprised; and that in itself was sad because you see, she would have made a far better Queen than her brother would have made a King. Ophir in those days was not the most enlightened of places, and truth be known, it was only a five day ride from T'eag, and T'eag has never in all it's long history ever had a ruling queen.

Jane left the palace the very day her brother was crowned. But she did not go without a plan. If there is one thing you have learned about Jane in all of this tale, then it is that she always had a plan.

She went first to the east vale, which was a very wealthy vale full of the richest and noblest families who farmed vast herds of sheep. It was the sheep and their shepherds that the dragon had been eating, remember. She told the rich landowners just how the emperor had been willing to leave the dragon ravaging the region and eating their livelihoods.

Then she went to the Great Green and spoke to the elves in their own tongue, for she had always been fascinated by the elves, and loved to learn about them. She told them how her brother had humiliated Baltoothis, Bera's own horse, by riding him in full panoply when he was trapped and unable to fight back.

And then she traveled to Channa and hunted down the son of the dead king. She married him and she and her husband returned to Ophir at the head of a vast army of elves, Channii and the mustered people of the east vale. She brought them to the gate of Ophir and laid the city under siege.

Now, you may think that Ham still had the horses that had been bred from Baltoothis. Indeed he still had Baltoothis himself, and he rode him proudly onto the field to meet his sister, though the horse was weighed down by chains and fifteen slaves held him tethered in a web of ropes so that he could barely move. Nevertheless, Ham still had the semi- divine, man-eating horses that had eaten the king of Channa.

A huge advantage!

Not really.

Because you see, the elves could speak horse and the horses could understand elf. The elves called to them and told them that they would ever be welcome in the Great Green where they could run free and eat whatever they liked; as long as it wasn't an elf.

Faced with an offer like that the green horses did what any self respecting horse would do, and deserted to the other side. Suddenly Ham was in a very precarious position, and he had the good sense to see it.

'Sister,' he called. 'It seems you have me at a disadvantage. You have an army and I have an empire. How shall we settle this?'

'Brother,' Jane called back.' You have Baltoothis, who is mine. A gift on our birthday. I would have him, and the empire.'

Now, it's possible that Jane had miscalculated here. For she had reminded Ham of the day he and his brothers had captured the horse and how Ham had been eaten. Ham smiled.

'Very well.' He said. 'I propose a challenge. The one of us who can ride Baltoothis longest without the weights holding him down or the web of ropes tethering him, gets both the horse and the empire. I'll even let you go first. How's that?' And that is the origin of the phrase 'Ladies First' which means a man wants a woman to deal with the danger before he has to.

'What a marvelous idea, Brother.' Jane called. 'I accept.'

Ham could hardly contain his delight. He was sure, you see, that Jane would get eaten, just like Ham had been.

But she didn't. The weights and the ropes were removed from Baltoothis and Jane approached him gently. She spoke to him in elvish, which he understood all too well, and she promised him that if he would only let her ride him for a moment then he would be set free to return to the Great Green. She also promised him that the very next person who tried to ride him after she had...he could eat.

And Baltoothis agreed. Jane pulled herself up into the saddle and rode the great animal in a walk about the field in front of her brother. Just for good measure she urged Baltoothis into a trot, a canter and a gallop as well. Then she dismounted and handed the reins to Ham.

'Your turn!' she said brightly.

Well, Ham's turn didn't go quite so well. In fact he smiled weakly up into Baltoothis's face and that's the origin of the saying 'Never look a gift horse in the mouth.' which means don't put your head near something that's hungry.

So, Jane became empress of the Channii Imperium and Ophir ceased to exist as a separate nation. Ty-Shour, the tangled god who sits at the root of all things, had finally had his revenge.

And that is the end of the tale of The Nine Princes of Ophir.

3

The Corpse Lay Deader

There was a hollow beneath the broken wall that provided pitiful shelter from the rain. Exhausted, Asquith dropped his pack. It landed with a sludgy thud in a puddle.

He would kill for a bit of fire. A Pile of dry wood. A handful of kindling. A spark. Bliss! But it would take a serious amount of magic to set any of the sodden wood he had managed to gather alight. Magic, serious or otherwise, was in short supply.

A crow blinked at him out of a stunted tree and ruffled rain from its feathers. That, he thought, was a good sign.

This had to be the place. He recalled the squint-eyed hag who had sold him the map. Well, *sold* was hardly the word. She clearly hadn't known what it was she had dangling from her belt. A few subtle questions, a few pleasantries and a copper coin or two and it was his.

He, of course, had spotted it instantly. Knew it for the treasure it was. He had seen pictures of it, remarkably accurate ones, in the ancient archives.

'Find the hill with two heads...' she had said in answer to his first question, which, he congratulated himself again, had been terribly subtle.

'I am researching ancient tomb carvings, and wondered if there might be any ancient tombs in the area?'

Masterfully obscure!

'Ooh, bless you, sir, but yes, the very most ancientest in all the world. It's "Hers", you know. That's what they say!' Her ragged voice dipped low and throaty as she pronounced the word 'Hers'.

'Hers?' he affected ignorance.

'The woman made of crows, herself. The Goddess of Death. Her tomb, if you can believe she needs one!' A sticky black drool of tobacco juice dribbled down her hairy chin. She sucked it back between her lips and presented him with a rictus grin that displayed grey gums and three blackened teeth. One of her eyes had a habit of looking down whilst the other looked up. Charmingly rustic!

'Really, you don't say.' He gifted her with his best smile.

Then, 'Oh, I say! What a delightful trinket!' His fingers fluttered over the copper tube at her waist. He could see the engravings, the intricate design. How it must have glowed once, the red-gold metal polished to a high shine. Now, though, it was cankered in green. Its lustre lost. Nevertheless, he could see the words upon it.

'Find me, choose your reward!'

What an invitation! Back in the Guild of Tomb Hunters in Carcamesh, they had speculated on the nature of the reward. To be fair, scholars had been speculating for a thousand years. Wealth, some hoped though most thought it must be eternal life, after all, what better gift could the goddess of death bestow? Well, Asquith didn't know, but here was the fabled artifact that would lead him to the answer. He could hardly believe his luck, to bump into this old hag and see it swinging between her legs. If he could get his hands on it...he was so close; maybe closer even than his own father had ever gotten.

He felt a sudden flush of bitter pride at that. That he might achieve the very thing that his father had been so obsessed with. This was, after all, the very reason his father had left all those years ago.

The quest to find the tomb of the woman made of crows had filled him to the brim, pushed out any iota of time or space to spare on a young son, or a lonely wife. It had eaten through the family wealth, isolated them from family and friends, left them all but destitute...and his father had never noticed, so focused was he on his quest.

There was an irony there that would have made Asquith smile, had he only been able to see past the burden his father's absence had placed upon his mother, how it had broken her spirit and ruined her health.

The only thing that kept his father alive was the search for the tomb of death.

Then one day he was gone, leaving only a note...

'I know where the map-key is...'

'What? This old thing?' The old hag's confused voice tore him back to the present and the disappearance of his father faded from his mind.

'Lady, no.' The woman grinned 'I found this sticking out of the mud aways up on the big hill, near the ruin. T'aint nothing but a gewgaw. Worth no more than a diddle and a fiddle.'

'Well, I think it quite remarkable and if you would oblige, I would like to pay you for it. What would you take?'

Of course, with no idea of its value she had undersold it. He tried hard to hide his smile. He handed her the coppers; the price of a dry crust in Carcamesh, but out here in the ragged hills it would probably buy several pigs, a goat, and all manner of comforts. In return she gave him the single most valuable artifact he had ever seen.

The map key to death's own tomb.

They would never believe it when he got home!

What a day!

'You mentioned an ancient tomb? Where would I find it?' he had asked.

'Up in the hills, away yonder' She waved absently over his shoulder. 'Find the hill with two heads.' She was sucking on the coins, trying to chew them with her rotten teeth. 'between the heads is a vale and in the vale you will find a wall, and in the wall there is a door; well, to say it's a door is to give it airs it doesn't deserve, it's more of a gash. You can't miss it. It moans, and the air that comes out of it is cold enough to freeze the best bits off a goat!'

It had taken him all day to find the hill with two heads, mainly because the rain clouds were so low that they covered the heads of all the hills around the village.

There were a lot of hills.

And here at last was the wall and the door; just as she had described. A tattered gash some three feet long and a few inches wide. It cut through the sandstone blocks like a sword cut through silk, and the wind that came out of it wailed like a soul in torment.

Just beneath it something slumped against the stone. He bent to examine it. A pack, not unlike his own but sodden and half rotten with mildew. Nearby was the ruin of a fire. Half blackened stumps of wood within a shallow scrape of soil. Had another come looking for the same treasure? It didn't matter. He had the one thing they could not have had. He had the map-key.

He pulled the copper cylinder from his pouch and felt for the line of folded metal that marked the scroll end. The tightly rolled parchment slid out with a dry sigh. Against the pale fabric dark lines of text were scratched, but in the gloom of evening the words were impossible to read. Rooting in his pack he found the mage glasses he had had the foresight to buy in Carcamesh. They slipped comfortably over the bridge of his nose and he fiddled the wire hooks into place behind his ears. These were the modern style. To anyone looking at him his eyes would be illuminated brilliant green and would look larger than they should. The mage who had made this particular pair had included a slight magnification spell into the lenses.

'It's all magical fashion!' the merchant had said with an insincere smile. 'last month mage glasses were red, next month they will probably be blue. That's the nature of fashion, it changes constantly. You never know where you are. Very good for trade, though.'

He shrugged the memory aside and brought the scroll up to his eyes.

'To open the way, sing the song that opens the way.'

What! all seventeen verses?

He cleared his throat and began to sing, his reedy voice rising and falling on the wind and in some uncanny way melding seamlessly with the melody that emanated from the gash in the wall. He sang the song of opening; the song that is sung to ease the journey of the departed through the Ninefold Gate to the blessed embrace of the woman made of crows. And as his ululating song died at the end of the seventeenth verse; the one where you promise to honour the goddess above all other gods, the gash in the wall reached out and sucked him into ...

***

...darkness. Cold, moist earth pressed into his face. He lay on a hard-packed floor that smelled of decay. Had the air been slightly warmer it would have been perfect for growing mushrooms. The glasses flickered back into life and he pushed himself to his feet. He was in a square room, each surface mirror smooth and intricately carved with lines of dark writing. In the light of the mage glasses he saw himself reflected back from each wall. There was no door, no gash through which he had entered.

Piles of earth and rot had gathered in the corners. He tried not to look too hard at them, they had the pale hue of mildewed bones. He pulled out the copper tube and read the second passage.

Five lives, nine gates. One life lost to reach this place.
To travel on you must survive
To claim the prize, reach the god alive...

Maybe he should have read the whole thing before he tried to enter! The remaining coil of paper was blank.

He cursed into the darkness. The polished walls cursed back.

There must be a way out, a hidden door or a secret passage; something. The verse said he could travel on. There must be a path to travel. He stepped up to the nearest wall; green light scattered across its smooth surface revealing the deeply engraved words. Unreadably old! He trailed his hands across the surface as he paced the perimeter of the room. The edges of the cuts were knife sharp beneath his fingers.

No doors. No switches and no clues. In fact, nothing except the hollow thud as he kicked something round out of tangled ivory sticks that had gathered in one corner. He watched the pallid ball tumble across the floor and settle. Not a ball. A skull. Rot toothed and hollow eyed. It grinned at him. Its eyes followed him as he completed the circuit of the walls.

Asquith had never considered himself to be a screamer, but he did have to concede that the acoustics in the small black room did wondrous things to the high pitched and timorous sound that erupted from his mouth when a dark shadow pulled itself from the mass of rot in the corner, the pile he had wanted to believe were just sticks. As the form shuffled into the green light his second scream was even less manly.

A man.

A man in mouldering leather armour. A corselet of rusted iron sagged about its knees and jangled as he moved.

A man with no face.

Well, he had a face; just no flesh on his face...and no lower jaw. Come to that it had no flesh at all to cover its yellowing bones. Asquith stifled a third scream and congratulated himself on how calm he felt as the cadaver stepped closer. It was dragging something behind it. Something heavy that needed both its skeletal hands to hold. Something that scraped across the floor with a dull, metallic grating sound. The creature twisted and swung its arms out. Asquith marvelled at how it moved without musculature. How its limbs managed to not only hold the heavy long sword, but to wield it as well. He watched with a detached fascination as the rusty length of iron arced over the corpses head; the dull, notched edge glinting in the emerald light as its weight carried it through the arc and down. He felt it strike his left shoulder. Felt it shatter bone and cleave flesh. Felt the cold heaviness of it slice into his chest and through his heart and, as his limbs lost the strength to hold him upright and his knees buckled, he thought to himself.

'Should have moved out the way!'

* * *

Life returned with a jolt and he sucked cool air into tight and empty lungs. He lay on a hard-packed floor that smelled of decay. Had the air been slightly warmer it would have been perfect for growing mushrooms. The glasses flickered back into life and he pushed himself to his feet. He was in a square room, each surface mirror smooth and intricately carved with lines of dark writing. In the light of the mage glasses he saw himself reflected back from each wall. There was no door, no gash through which he had entered.

Piles of earth and rot had collected in the corners. He tried not to look too hard at them, they had the pale hue of mildewed bones. He pulled out the copper tube and read the second passage.

Five lives, nine gates. One life lost to reach this place.
One life lost to iron blade...

Maybe he should have read the whole thing before he tried to enter! He pulled the parchment further from its tube. The remaining coil of paper was blank.

A chill tickled down his spine. There was something terribly familiar with the last five minutes. Had he dreamed them? Had he read them somewhere?

He cursed into the darkness. The polished walls cursed back. Then he cursed again as he realised the meaning of the passage. No. He had lived them already.

Eight gates still to traverse and three lives left. What would happen if he ran out of lives?

He peered into the mirror smooth walls and there, in the

shadows behind him he saw a shape shuffling forwards dragging a sword. Jawless mouth grinning and empty eye sockets leering. Asquith stepped backwards. Something on the floor grabbed at him. He looked down. A mass of pale white bone; a grinning skull. The hard, grey sharpness of a blade.

That hadn't been there before. Was that fresh blood on the blade?

The cadaver was in front of him. It shifted, throwing its weight...what was left of it...into a swing . Asquith rolled aside as the blade came down. It struck the bone pile, shattering the ancient ivory to dust and rang like a broken bell as it connected with the floor. The vibration that ran up the blade was too much for the cadaver. Bones disintegrated. Dried and brittle connective tissue snapped and flaked, and the body collapsed into a heap on the floor. Asquith caught the sword as it fell, it was cold in his hands and heavy.

Then he fell through the floor.

***

Water. Deep and cold and fast covered him, flowing into his nose and mouth. The sword pulled him down, dragging him deeper and deeper into the torrent.

'I can't drown...three lives left...only two rooms in...' he dropped the sword just as his feet slammed into a hard, stone surface. He must be dozens of feet underwater! Bracing his knees, he pushed for the surface. Freed from the weighty weapon he soared.

Air. Sweet, sweet air rushed into his lungs as he broke through the surface.

He found himself in a vast open hall. Great lanterns hung

from the high ceilings, their light casting across row after row of wooden shelving that disappeared into the heights above him and on every shelf; books. Thousands and thousands of books and scrolls and tablets. There were tables as well, each piled high with dusty volumes and about the huge shadowed room, shapes shuffled. Robed and hooded figures pacing endlessly between the shelves, reverently touching the books. Almost before he knew it his hand had plucked one from the top of a pile.

'*The History of the March of the Dead.*' Impossible. That was a book that had been lost since the fall of the star that had erased T'iu from the world. The next book in the pile drew his eye.

'*The Book of The Night Walker.*' Even more impossible than the existence of the first book. This one written by the dead god Ourano in the days before his death. A series of prophecies. No copy had ever been found.

What he could learn from these books. He hurried to another table, pulling tome after tome. Books full of maps of lands lost to the sea. Histories of the war between the gods, books of tales of Meura and Bera, Aiasier and Velvet Schem. So much knowledge he felt almost giddy to see it. Why, in a single day he could learn enough from just one of them to rewrite the history of the world.

Where to start.

As he walked deeper and deeper into the room, he became aware of something else.

A great round doorway occupied one entire wall of the library, and before it another figure. This one dressed in a ragged robe. A hood covered its face, but the fire that kindled in its eyes revealed skull features and in its skeletal hands it held a long shaft of ebony topped with a silver star.

A mage!

To be accurate a dead mage!

No. An un-dead mage.

He knew how to kill mages. He also knew how mages killed you.

'Never run away from a mage who is about to throw a spell at you. Fatal. I have seen more hunters killed by running away than I've had hot barmaids. Mage magic needs time to weave. They can't just fling out spells, they must construct them. Running just gives them more time to weave and take aim. Get in close before they can strike...'

One of the more exciting books on tomb raiding. He had enjoyed that one.

The mage was already weaving. The lines of power were invisible, but he could taste the magic building. Asquith ran screaming at the undead mage. He saw the spell begin to burn around the silver pommel of the staff. A spear of fire shot towards him and he dropped, sliding across the polished floor as the incandescent fire passed over his head and then his momentum slammed him into the mage's flesh-less legs.

Bone snapped. Thankfully not his. The mage tottered and fell, the sodden rotting mass of its body landing heavily on the floor. Asquith snatched up the staff and brought it down sharply on the hooded head. Bone cracked.

The corpse lay dead...no...the corpse lay deader.

He swallowed the giggle that bubbled up from his gut. He took a moment to lean on the staff and look at his victim; little more than a pillow of rotting fabric .

What was that dangling from the mages belt? A cankerous green tube of copper. The cord that held it to the belt parted rottenly as he pulled it away. He turned it in his fingers. The small engravings were the same, the fold of copper that held the parchment was the same. Even the curious little dent in the side...Identical. He pulled and the scroll unrolled and fell to mildewed mush.

A second map key! His fingers fumbled at his own belt, found the solid hardness of his own map key in its pouch and pulled it into the green light.

Had the old hag duped him? Did she have some production line in the back of her hovel? Impossible! He felt suddenly lightheaded. He leaned back against the closed door and found there was nothing to lean on. The path had once again opened for him to follow.

He glanced back towards the acres of books and the knowledge and history they contained. Then he tossed the mage's ruined map key onto the mage's corpse, and turned his back on the library and stepped through the door.

History was one thing, but this was exciting...

* * *

Gold. Everything was gold. And jewels! So many jewels. Piles of them. Mounds of rubies like frozen hills of blood. Emeralds so green it seemed the ocean had been turned to stone. Pearls, lustrous and pure; buckets of them. And tables of the most exotic and delicious food.

So much wealth. And beyond it all an open doorway leading further in. A giggle of delight fell off his lips. He ran to a pile of ice white diamonds. They felt cold and sharp and crystal hard as he plunged his hands in.

What could he do with all of this wealth?

For a start, he would never be cold again. Never be hungry.

That dank little cell where he slept, five levels below the street and barely above the level of the water table so that on days of heavy rain he would wake to swing his feet into ankle deep and freezing water; well, that would be gone. Let some other novice suffer the damp and the slime and the cold. He could buy a palace...one of those magnificent ones on the banks of the third circle, with acres of gardens, orchards of fruiting trees, high and airy rooms and hot running water!

All those jeers he had suffered as a child, the taunts from the other boys whose fathers had not abandoned them...this would buy the respect he truly deserved...and well...he could fund his own library...his own hall of learning...By Ty-Shours twisted testicles, he could build his own university, then those anemic, pinch-faced and narrow-minded deans and lore-masters would have to come bowing, caps in hand, to him for the funds and the permissions to begin their researches.

He would have that most elusive of all things...respect.

A whole new world of possibilities opened before his eyes, and he felt a laugh of purest joy bubble through him.

But, as he filled his pocket's he became aware of a dull rumble and looking up he was in time to see the door close with a soft 'click'.

Asquith sighed and dropped the diamonds back onto the pile. The door clicked again and began to open.

He picked up a stone and the door closed a fraction.

He dropped the stone and the door opened a sliver.

Asquith cursed into the sparkling air and emptied his pockets of more wealth than he could ever dream of.

As each stone plinked back onto the pile the door teased open a shade wider.

Empty-handed, Asquith stalked towards the door.

Now he saw that he was not alone. Six figures sat at the groaning table. Cadaverous and skeletal their heads turned to watch him as he stalked. But they did not stand. Instead they protectively pulled great piles of wealth away from him.

He paused as he passed, his eyes taken by a dull greening copper tube hanging from the belt of one of the corpses...so like the one that he had purchased from the hag...were these hunters, just like him?

If he had lacked the strength to discard the stones, would he have joined them at the table, unable to progress...stuck here for eternity?

Another thought slid, worm-like into his mind. Had his father found the old hag? Could it be that he had also found the map key?

'*I know where it is...*' He had said. Could he be here, somewhere in this maze...

Asquith found himself studying the dry and stretched faces of the guests seated at the table, searching for some familiar feature; anything that might tell him who they were. But their skin was brittle and shrunken and dry and their features warped and sunken...

There was a joke here, he thought. The woman made of crows was laughing, why had he ever thought she would just let people wander into her tomb without consequence?

'Why had no-one thought this would be dangerous...' He thought. 'She would not make this easy.'

He needed time to think, time to take a breath and get his mind in order. But since the gash in the wall had pulled him inside, the path had been relentless. He had stepped from one challenge to another without respite, and this was certainly no place to linger. The smells of the food had awoken his stomach. It growled and his mouth watered.

One bite of a delicious pie, a sip of aromatic wine...would that trap him here?

He could not take the risk. He turned away and staggered through the door.

* * *

Now, this was more like it. This looked like a chamber in an ancient tomb. Sandstone walls and a floor made of granite blocks. Great pillars; gaudily painted in blues and greens held up a ceiling painted to resemble stars. The walls were lined with statues of the gods. He knew them all, of course. Bera, hunched and ancient, a cunning smile carved on thin and twisted lips. Meura, dressed in water, a chain of fish about her neck. Velvet Schem, cloaked and unknowable. A cat at her feet, watching him with sapphire eyes. Ty-Shour, tentacle headed, sitting on his throne of bone. Aiasier, palms out holding dancing flames. He had no face within his crown of hair, just a blazing fire. And then the dead ones. their alcoves in shadow. At the end of the hall was the woman made of crows. Standing taller than all the rest. A liberty, he thought, seeing as she wasn't even one of the major nine. She was carved of black stone, her dress like feathers and her face pale and angular with bead-like eyes and a blade of a nose. Three crows perched on her outstretched arm. He knew their names. Ruatha, the bird of tomorrow. Buatha, the bird of yesterday, and Amatha, the bird of today. He had studied these birds. They had, in a way, led him here.

Then as he put one foot down, the world tilted; not enough to pitch him forwards, but enough to make him stop. To throw out his arms for balance and to pray. He looked down. The slab he stood on was poised on an angle. Through the slot that had opened behind him he could see a dizzying fall. There were marks on the granite at the very edge of the lip, where the fall awaited. Little collections of scrapes and grooves...like the scratches left by finger-nails?

No, they couldn't be...whose nails were tough enough to scratch granite? He laughed at the absurdity of the notion and the floor shuddered.

He felt himself slip towards the drop and he became aware that something other than the blank-eyed gods was watching him. There was a creature standing on the opposite lip of the slab. Small and gangly and malformed; as if the goddess had taken a crow and a cat and a spider and squeezed them together. It tilted its head to fix him with one beady black eye. A long pink tongue flicked across its lips.

Asquith knew this creature's name. The one who weighed the worth of the dead. There was no running from Methucas. The creature moved forwards with a curious scuttling gait and the floor shivered again, opening the gap beneath him wider, but Asquith did not really notice. There was something hypnotic in the way Methucas moved, and in his piercing gaze. He didn't move even when the creature began to climb up his legs, or when it clamped its hand-like paws against his head and fixed its broad feathery lips to his, and wormed its impossibly long tongue between his teeth and down his throat.

He woke in a pool of cold urine on a floor that was mercifully un-tilted. His head ached and his mouth stung with the acidic taste of bile and something else that he did not want to think had been left behind by the invading tongue. Images hung behind his eyes...and he heard his own voice, replaying his history...things he had said, things he had done...the residue of Methucas's study. That's what Methucas existed for, to measure the worth of those on the path of the dead.

Asquith felt himself go suddenly cold.

'Am I dead?'

He had to be dead if Methucas was measuring his worth...he pulled out the scroll and read the lines. No change, but that in itself did not answer the question.

Asquith took in one long shuddering breath, and looked up into the eyes of the statue of the woman made of crows. She looked impassively back, but one of the crows on her outstretched arm seemed to blink at him.

'I want to go back...' He stammered...'Can I go back?'

His voice echoed, but there was no answer. Not even from the crow. He hadn't really expected one.

The statues of the gods looked down. They seemed less interested now than they had been. He glanced back the way he had come. No door, just a richly painted plaster wall and a granite floor covered in the desperate claw marks of others who had flailed against the drop. Just one way, then. Forward through the door that stood open between the legs of the goddess of death.

He felt soiled. Well he was soiled. As he stood, he realised he had done more than piss himself. He threw a curse at the gods and imagined laughter on their cold stone lips as he hobbled splay-legged through the fourth gate.

* * *

The door ground shut behind him and plunged him into utter darkness. The mage glasses fizzed and puffed, and the light flickered on, then off, then on. In the brief sparks of flickering light, he saw where he stood.

A hole. Vast and black. So huge that he could see neither roof nor walls. There was no floor, just vertiginous deeps on either side of the narrowest of narrow paths that opened from the end of the passage and twisted away into darkness. He had seen gypsy entertainers dancing and tumbling on ropes strung at head height above a crowd. This path was wider, but giddyingly high. He dropped a coin into the void. He waited for the clunk of its landing. And waited. And waited some more. Silence. The mage glasses gave one last disconsolate gasp and died, and the door he had walked through crept up behind him and pushed him into the void.

His scream as he fell into the endless deep, was long and protracted and ended with a sickening, and quite painful, thud-splat-crunch -crack...

* * *

The door ground shut behind him and plunged him into utter darkness. The mage glasses fizzed and puffed, and the light flickered on, then off, then on...

No time to waste.

He fumbled for the tube and unrolled the parchment. In the flickering light of the glasses the words danced. His heart was still as he read them.

Five lives, nine gates. One life lost to reach this place.
One life lost to iron blade.
One life lost to the endless deep...

* * *

Two lives left. Four gates. He felt the door creeping up behind him and stepped out onto the path. The glasses sighed and died.

He shuffled rather than stepped. One foot feeling the slender path, finding balance, settle his weight, drag the following foot, shift his weight back.

Slide

Balance

Drag

Repeat

At first, his eyes played tricks on him. He imagined shapes were drifting up from the black void. Glowing figures who might have resembled people he had known. People he had lost. Some cried, silently. Others beckoned for him to join them.

Slide

Balance

Drag

Repeat

Was that his mother? Sad the way she had died. He had tried to cry, but his work had consumed him. A sudden flush of guilt shuddered through him. He hadn't even visited her grave! He felt himself waver on the path. The dizzying deeps pulled at him. So easy just to let himself fall. He closed his eyes against the ghosts. His own darkness was preferable to the darkness he felt flooding his heart.

Slide

Balance

Drag

Repeat.

* * *

Wind. Strong and dry and hot, like standing in front of an open furnace. The ground was soft and shifted beneath his questing foot. He opened his eyes, and immediately slammed them closed against bright sunlight.

He stood on the lip of a high dune on the edge of a sea of sand that rolled away in all directions. There was nothing else. Nothing except him.

What was he supposed to do here? There was no path to follow. No clue as to which direction he should walk. He slumped onto the dune and watched the slicks of sand trickle down the steep side. Something white appeared as the sand shifted, bleached like ivory, tatters of bronze rags clung to it. Curiously Asquith brushed it clean.

A hand; or it had been once. It was closed around a small green copper cylinder. He pulled it from the dead grip and unrolled the brittle parchment. The words on it vanished in dusty fragments as the wind took them.

'Well, sitting here didn't do you much good!' he muttered to the bones. His voice sounded strange to his ears. He hadn't spoken to a living soul since he had found the map. He thought of the figures who had arisen from the void; thought about the aching guilt he had felt. And he spoke into the wind.

'I am sorry, mother.' He whispered. 'That I was not there for you...' When she wrapped her arms about him, he was hardly surprised. He looked into her familiar smile, so full of love and acceptance that his lack of thought for her suffering, his own selfishness for a career that was more important even than her, all but broke his heart.

'It is not from me that you need to find forgiveness!' Her voice was a rustle of sand across the dune. 'It is from yourself!'

Together they walked into the desert, hand in hand. He and his mother's ghost.

* * *

More wind. Bitterly cold and full of biting snow that stung his face like a million angry bees. Behind him black rock pressed into his back and loomed above him. He looked down. His feet were planted on a narrow snow-covered ledge. Between his toes, a void of swirling white and a sheer face of rock descending forever. A mountain then.

He pulled out the map and unrolled it with fingers so numb that it felt as if he was using someone else's. The scroll fluttered in the wind as he read. It recorded no further deaths. Still two lives and two more gates.

His mother had stayed with him as he walked through the desert. Sometimes others had joined them. People he had not thought of for years. Some he hardly recognised. People he had failed, people he had avoided. They talked, and he listened and gradually it occurred to him how hollow was his life, how focused on himself he had been.

She was gone now. They all were. He felt himself alone again, and his loneliness felt heavy. Where now? Clearly either right or left. There were no other options. He shuffled right, into the teeth of the biting wind. The cold ripped at him; became blades that cut to his bones. His breath turned to ice and caked his lips and his fingers and toes burned with frozen fire. He pushed on against the rattle in his head that told him to go back. The other path would be easier.

She would not make this easy.

Thirty steps on, and an hour later he shuffled round the curve of the mountain. Two paths now. One leading down. Through the billowing storm he saw a gentle slope descend to snow covered trees, green valleys, and a rushing river. He turned his back on paradise and took the ascending path into the mouth of the wind.

She would not make this easy.

His blood was ice. It creaked and cracked in his veins as he moved, one inch at a time. With each straining breath he sucked in the thin air and the world span about him, but he pushed on upwards and until there was nothing left to climb. Just the velvet sky and the diamond stars. He sat heavily and closed his eyes.

* * *

Five lives, nine gates. One life lost to reach this place.

One life lost to iron blade.

One life lost to the endless deep.

One life lost to frozen sleep...

The parchment scrolled back into its tube with a click that was torn away by the biting wind. Between his feet the dizzying drop opened invitingly. Asquith shuffled right.

He was so close. All he had to do was stay awake!

One life and two gates left.

She would not make this easy.

* * *

The second time he summited the mountain he stayed awake as the stars turned overhead and his breath came ragged in the thin air.

Nothing changed.

The cold seeped through his skin and into his bones and as he breathed he felt it turn his lungs to ice. Overhead the sky turned, the moon rose, casting silver light to reflect off the snow and blind his ice grimed eyes, and he wondered if he should have turned left...or taken the downward path to the tree filled vale.

* * *

His nerves were on fire. The tips of his fingers burned, his toes were agony, his face felt raw...but he was alive...

A white room. So white that for a moment he thought he must still be on the snow covered mountain, but this was a warm, womb of a room. Two doors stood opposite, and beside each stood a figure. Human in shape but with the head of a crow.

They watched him silently through bead black eyes and he realised that these were alive, not statues, not corpses...these were living things.

'Err...hello!' He said.

They said nothing.

'These are the guardians.' A voice seemed to whisper out of nowhere. 'One tells only lies, the other only truth. One door leads to what you seek, the other leads to your deepest nightmare. Ask one question and choose.'

'A riddle!' Asquith laughed. 'After all that, a riddle!'

Silence, and the beady gaze of the crow-headed guardians.

Well, he had beaten every other test the woman made of crows had placed before him. The warrior with his sword, the mage, the room of temptation, the testing of Methucas, the balanced path, the trackless waste, and the mountain. He could beat this riddle just as easily.

He pulled himself to his feet and with tentative, tingling steps he approached the nearest of the guardians. It was taller then he had thought it was. It towered over him so that it had to tilt its black feathered head to peer across its beak at him with glittering eyes. Asquith threw it a self conscious smile and a tiny wave.

'Um...' he said. He opened his mouth to say *'Just one question?'* but shut it before he could utter the words. He felt his face flush at the stupidity of almost asking one question to clarify that he could only ask one question.

'If I were to ask the other guardian which door leads to the goal I seek...' he murmured with infinite care, 'Which door would they indicate?'

The crow-headed man blinked slowly and raised a scaled and clawed hand to indicate the door to it's left. Asquith nodded.

'If you are the guardian who lies.' Asquith said, thoughtfully. 'Then your companion is the one who only tells the truth. As you are the guardian who only lies, then you are lying when you tell me he would indicate the left hand door. That means that the right hand door is the door that leads to my goal.' He nodded to himself, satisfied with the logic of his deduction.

'But, if you are the guardian who only tells the truth, that means that your companion is the one who only lies. As I asked which door leads to my goal, he would show me the door that leads to my deepest nightmare. You, being the guardian of truth would know this and show me which door he would indicate. That means that the left hand door can only be the one that leads to my deepest nightmare, and the right hand door leads me to my goal.'

Asquith smiled. 'All I have to do is step through?'

But of course, no one answered.

With a deep breath, he pulled himself up to his full height, dusted down his ragged clothes, and stepped through the door on the right.

* * *

He found himself back on the side of a mountain, but this time it was not so high, and not covered in drifts of freezing snow. Instead he was in a clearing amongst tall, stately trees. Overhead dark, clear skies carried a thousand stars and in the centre of the clearing a small campfire crackled and sparked within a circle of stones. A woman sat beside it, poking at the fire with a metal shod staff.

She looked up as Asquith appeared.

'Welcome.' She said. 'You've come a long way.'

'I...er...' Asquith began, but his words trailed away as he recognised her. Not so bent, not so decrepit and not so charmingly rustic, maybe...but he recognised the old woman who had sold him the map-key.

'You!' He whispered. She nodded.

'Me.'

'Who are you, is this a trick?' Asquith asked confused.

'Now then. ' Said the woman, 'that's two questions, and the answer to both is the same. Come, sit beside my fire and warm your bones; the ice must still be in there, I think.' She patted the log she sat on and shuffled sideways to make room for him.

'The answer, ' She smiled, and the light of the fire glanced off the hard angles of her cheeks and the sharpness of her nose and made her bead black eyes dance, 'rather depends on what you expected to find at the end, and what you thought you would gain from the finding of it!' She winked at him, and her thin, blood-red lips curled in a quizzical look. Asquith gasped, remembering the blade-like nose of the statue of the goddess of death and thinking that this woman's nose seemed remarkably blade-like itself.

'Well...' he murmured. 'There was mention of a reward...'

'I don't think that was it.' The woman said. 'If you had only been interested in a reward then the hall of temptation would have stopped you, as it stopped so many others.'

'But I would have died in there?'

She shrugged. 'Well, you were already dead, so technically you would have rotted in there. But you would have been rich!'

'That seems an unfair bargain.'

'Life...' she murmured sagely, 'is rarely fair. So, you did not come for reward, then what?'

'Knowledge...I suppose.' he murmured, but she shook her head.

'The library.' She said. 'All the knowledge in the world, and you turned your back on it with nary a glance, even though you knew there were books in there that you had never read and would never be able to find again. That's where your father ended. He couldn't get past the books. A shame, I had high hopes for him.'

Asquith felt his breath stop. His father had found the gate. It made for a strange feeling to know that he had followed in his father's footsteps, even that he had surpassed him.

'Does that give you peace?' She asked. 'To know how your father ended? It must do, I suppose, he has tormented you your whole life with his absence.

Why did he leave?

Why did he never return?

Well now you know. Though he was a mage, and powerful, he was, in the end, weaker than you. He fell to the temptation of knowledge.'

'He was looking for the woman made of crows.' Asquith whispered. She laughed and shook her head.

'Then he was a fool. He didn't have to come searching for me, everyone meets me eventually. It's about the only certainty in life.'

'He followed the clues you left. We both did.' Asquith snapped. 'You led us here...you're the reason he left when I was a child.'

'I left the map key, laid the clues that led you to it.' The woman made of crows replied. 'But I did not make either of you follow them. Something inside you did that.'

'He got stuck in the library?' Asquith demanded. 'Is he still in there?'

'Yes.'

'Was he the one I faced?' Asquith asked in a very small voice. 'Was he the one who tried to kill me?'

She glanced at him for a moment and the sly smile slid slightly from her lips.

'There is a possessiveness to some scholars, you know.' she murmured. 'Some of them will guard a hoard of knowledge more tenaciously than a dwarf guards a seam of gold.'

'That's not an answer.'

'Yes it is, it just is not the answer you wanted.'

'Can you get him out?'

'Of course I can, but why would I? He came to complete a quest and he failed. Failure has consequences. Unless...' She smiled. '...as you say, I promised a reward if you found me. Is that the reward you want? Your father back? That's easy.'

Asquith was nodding before he realised it. 'And my mother.' He muttered. The woman made of crows laughed again, this time with delight.

'One is a reward.' She said. 'Two is a price. You still have not answered my question. What were you hoping to find at the end, and what did you hope to gain from the finding of it? You said knowledge, but we have established that it was not knowledge you sought. Try again.'

Asquith thought for a long moment as the fire crackled and crows bickered in the trees about him and the wind began to moan through the branches.

'Adventure?' He suggested. 'I kind of just wanted to see what was at the end...'

'You just kind of wanted to see what was at the end.' She repeated. 'So you threw yourself into the pit to see what would happen?'

Now that she said it, Asquith felt suddenly self-conscious. Was that what he'd done? He had always known people who did things like that. Bennar was always climbing things without ropes to keep him safe, he'd climbed one of the mage towers once, all the way to the top.

'Why do you do it?' he had asked him once. Bennar had laughed.

'Because it's there, and because I can.'

Then Shand, he'd taken a job trapping bears...BEARS...and all manner of dangerous beasts. He needed them alive because he sold them on to soul eaters; and a soul eater needed a living creature to extract a soul from. Shand had always claimed it wasn't dangerous, but a bear was a bear and they ate anything, including people.

Then he thought of all the people from the Guild of Tomb Hunters, all the ones who had gone off hunting for things, and never come back...like his father. He'd heard stories from other tomb hunters. Gessick had claimed he had found the corpse of a hunter trapped in a chamber deep beneath a howe somewhere in T'eag, the woman had somehow locked the door behind her and died trying to dig her way out with her bare hands. He'd never really believed the story, Gessick was always being morbid like that, but he hadn't slept well for a long while after he had heard it.

He shrugged.

'Am I dead?'

The woman laughed.

'Of course you're dead.' She grinned. 'If there's one thing you must know about the nine fold gate, the living may not pass in and the dead may not pass out. You died the moment the gash in the wall pulled you in. I'm frankly surprised you have to ask, how big was the gash? a few feet long and a few inches wide.' She gave him an appraising look. 'You are considerably more than a few inches wide, you should be thankful that it was quick and the dead remember no pain... but that's really not important. We can change that at any time, if you want...' She peered at him sidelong, her eyes twinkled and her mouth twisted in a wry smile. 'But I don't think you want to die. You asked if you could stop, didn't you. Asked if you could just go back.' Asquith nodded, glumly.

'Well, you couldn't go backwards. Once you're on the path, you're on the path, for good or ill.' She poked the fire again, sending flights of embers twisting into the air. 'But you had every opportunity to just let it all end really, by just running out of lives, but something in here stopped you, didn't it.' A long, black scaled and clawed finger reached up poked his forehead, right between his eyes. 'Made you fight, made you struggle on. I like that. It's what I'm looking for.'

'You're her, aren't you.' Asquith breathed. 'The woman made of crows...' She threw him another wink.

'That I am. Again, I am surprised, you demonstrated a quick wit before my guardians, I would have thought you a tad quicker on the uptake...but I suppose you have been through an ordeal...' She said.

'As it happens, I have need of someone with your particular skill set. Someone who is focused,clever, brave, resourceful, dependable, and cannot be distracted from their task. There's something I need you to do for me.'

'And if I do it you will return my father?'

'Have I not said that I will return him anyway? I promised a reward.' She laughed. 'Do this simple task for me, and I will return your mother also. That is my price.'

'Is it dangerous?'

'Well, I'm the goddess of death, so if you are worried about dying...you needn't be.' said the woman made of crows. Asquith felt himself nodding.

'What is it you want me to do?'

'High in the mountains on the other side of the world, there is a hidden city.' She said. 'And deep beneath it there is a...tomb... hidden and lost. I want you to open it. That's all. Open it and let the thing inside, out. Can you do that?'

'That actually doesn't sound too hard.' Asquith murmured. 'What do I get for doing it?'

* * *

'Is that what I think it is?' Ratch asked, breathlessly. His fingers reached out to gently touch the little cankered copper tube the old woman held in her gnarled fingers.

'Why, dearie, that all depends..' The woman grinned, displaying rotting teeth and a fat pink tongue. 'On what you think it is?'

'I think it's the map key to the tomb of the carrion queen!'

Ratch whispered.

'Then, yes.' The hag's grin grew wider. 'That's exactly what it is. Do you want it? It's yours for a price...'

4

How Bera Reclaimed her Gift

There are things in the Great Wood that have no great love for man, and chief of these is Bera...

If you have ever wondered how the endless war between men and elves started, then let me tell you.

It all began long, long ago before the world bore the names we now recognise. It began with a wedding. The marriage of the daughter of the King of Avalor to the King of Chun.

Chun was a wealthy kingdom and powerful. Richer, it has to be said, and certainly more powerful than Avalor. But, almost as some commentary on the ephemeral nature of humanity, both are lost now; destroyed long ago in the war that followed. There are ruins in the deserts of Chu, great piles of carved stone and forests of pillar bases that some scholars say is all that is left of the great temple of Chun.

This temple was consecrated to the glory of Bright Aiasier, the lord of the sky and the vault of heaven, but it was so perfect in form and so beautiful to look upon that it became famous for being just itself. Aiasier, as he always did, demanded a spectacular temple, and the people of Chun, who were devout, gave him exactly what he asked for.

It was a thousand feet long and six hundred feet wide and stood as high as six tall buildings. Its walls were clad in stone and carved in the most intricate designs with the stories of the life of the Great God, and the carvings were coated in beaten gold so that the whole temple shone in the sunlight like a star that had been brought to earth. It was so tall, and so bright that it could be seen for a dozen leagues, and even ships out in the sun-swallowing sea used it as a beacon to find their way to the port of Chun.

You are probably wondering why I am describing a temple, when I promised to tell you how a war began. Well; it's important, so hold your questions and listen on.

Inside, the temple was just as beautiful. A thousand carved bases of great pillars were spaced in great concentric circles, and on each base a massive wooden pillar was placed to hold up the carved and painted ceiling. These pillars were Great oaks, which Bera herself had given to Chun for the express purpose of building this very temple. They came from her own sacred groves deep in the core of the Green Heart, the very centre of her realm. It is said that, though they were cut down and carved into forms; each still retained the living soul of the tree it had once been. They whispered constantly of the glory and greatness of the Lord of Heaven so that the temple was always full of praise for Aiasier.

Now it so happened that it was in this temple that the wedding of the King of Chun to the Princess of Avalor took place.

You should know that the king of Avalor had no love for his new son-in-law. Indeed, his jealousy of him knew no bounds.

He hated the fact that this man had won the heart of his

beloved daughter.

He envied his wealth which was so much greater than the wealth of Avalor.

He hated his beauty and his prowess for he was still young and still virile, and that just reminded the king of Avalor of all the things he had lost...or had never had.

He despised the city of Chun for its graceful architecture and wide avenues, its gardens and its high walls which had never been breached by any army. Indeed, it was everything that Avalor was not.

Above all he was jealous of the wonderous temple that the King of Chun, and the people of his city took so much for granted.

The King of Avalor vowed to himself, as he sat in that golden shrine listening to his beloved daughter reciting her wedding vows as the trees of Bera's grove whispered their adoration and devotion to the Lord of the Sky and the Vault of Heaven, that he would see a greater temple built in Avalor or die in the attempt.

Had that been the end of it then things might have turned out differently. The King of Avalor could have returned to his own kingdom bitter and angry and he could have quietly forgotten his internal vow.

But, that evening, as the guests gathered to celebrate the marriage, and the wine and mead flowed and the King of Chun became more and more generous and the King of Avalor became drunker and drunker and more bitter with every gift, things took a decidedly more spiteful turn.

The King of Avalor stood, a mite unsteadily for the golden honey wine he had been drinking was powerful stuff, and banged his goblet on the table for silence.

"I want to thank you, my Lord King, for your unceasing largess, your hospitality and your great honour in marrying my dear daughter!" there was a wave of polite muttering. So far, so good, though many in the crowd would have preferred a tad less sharpness in his tone; and was that sarcasm they could detect? Surely the King of Chun had been all of the things that had been stated...they had all witnessed it.

" And I want to tender my own invitation!" The King of Avalor waved his goblet in the air, sloshing very expensive wine over the guests nearest to him. "To all of you here today, To you, the Queen of Lish, and you the King of Lughannn, and even to you, the Prince of Myacar, though your princedom is small and not very important. In one year and one day I will hold a celebration of the first anniversary of this glorious wedding. In my own temple to Velvet Schem we will hold a grand blessing to this union!"

"But Father" said the new Queen of Chun, slightly anxiously, for she knew her father well, and had cause to worry that he was over reaching. "There is no temple to Velvet Schem in Avalor!"

"Then I will damn well build one!" the king of Avalor roared "And it will be a darned sight more impressive than that over done hay barn you got married in!"

"Father..." the Queen of Chun began, but her husband stopped her with a gentle hand on her arm.

"We accept!" he said. "In one year and one day we will come to Avalor to celebrate the blessing of our marriage in your new temple. A temple for the goddess of the moon to stand beside my own temple to her consort, the lord of the sun. I can think of nothing more appropriate. Would you like me to do anything to help you get the building off the ground? Lend you some craftsmen, I have very good stone masons, and some highly experienced goldsmiths...though for a temple to the moon I would suppose you might need silversmiths. Maybe a few masters of stained glass. I could lend you some money at a very reasonable rate..."

"I don't need anything from you..." snorted the king of Avalor.

Well. That was it. The damage was done. The challenge laid, and the inevitable disastrous end ordained. There might as well have been a demonic peel of thunder and a supernatural giggle.

Truth be known, the marriage of the Princess of Avalor to the King of Chun was a wonderful thing for Avalor. An alliance between these two cities created opportunities for trade, which Avalor needed desperately. Avalor was not a powerful kingdom and it was surrounded by avaricious enemies, the most powerful of which was Rogar. The Rogan had for many years raided deeply into Avalor and killed and enslaved many people. Now, with this single marriage, Rogar sat precariously with Avalor on its southern border, and powerful Chun on its western border. This was an exceptional strategic match; but the very best politics can be undone by the hubris of man.

Avalor was not a city like Chun. It was moderately rich, but it had no vast wealth and no vast resources. It was built on a parcel of land gifted to the founder of the city by Bera herself, the Mother of Beasts, the Green Queen, the goddess of the wild.

Why Bera gifted part of her own Green Heart to the founder of Avalor is an interesting tale, but it does not come into this one, so we will not mention it again. It is enough for you to know that Avalor could grow no more, for it already filled the gift and was now hard pressed on three sides by the great trees of the Green Heart, and on the fourth by the nation of Rogar.

As soon as he returned home the King of Avalor summoned his chief architect to order the construction of the temple. When the old man heard what was demanded of him, he went as white as a sheet, clutched hard at his chest, and dropped dead on the spot. The king looked at the architect's assistant and said.

"It will take too long to get a new chief architect; congratulations. You are promoted. Get me preliminary designs by the end of the week. Remember, this temple must put the one in Chun into the shade; in every conceivable way. If you succeed, you can name your price. If you fail I will throw you off the roof!"

The assistant, now Chief Architect of Avalor, was no fool. In fact, he probably wished he too could drop dead on the spot, but that didn't happen.

"But my Lord!" he said "Where will I build this temple? There is no space in the city, in fact a temple such as you request would cover more land than there is within the walls of Avalor itself!"

Now that was a very good question. Where could the King of Avalor build his great temple?

Now, the new chief architect was an intelligent, but ambitious young man, and currently his ambitions ran to not being thrown off the roof of a disappointing temple. He knew, as I am sure you also know, that a temple the size of the one the King of Avalor demanded could never be built within a single year; it was quite impossible.

He left his audience with the king in a terrible depression. He wandered the shadowed streets of Avalor and as he did so his mind played over a single question.

What could he do?

What could he do?

Now, you are no doubt thinking that flight was upper most in his mind, and it was, it's true. He was considering how he could escape the city and find a way to a place of safety, when his feet, quite of their own accord, brought him to the doors of another temple. Until the kings sudden inspiration to build a vast new shrine to the goddess of the moon, this temple had been the largest and most magnificent in all of Avalor. It's dark and sinuous walls and the great liquid eyes of the octopus-like being who peered at him from the bronze doors proclaimed this the shrine to Ty-Shour, the tangled god who sits at the root of all things. If there is one god amongst all the gods who dislikes Bera more, then they are hard to find.

We have reached the part of the story where we need to make a slight detour to consider the nature of Gods.

They are jealous.

They do not like others touching their things.

They most certainly do not like mortals taking liberties.

They are capricious, like the weather they can change in a moment.

They are devious. Their deals are rigged always in their own favour, and though they may seem to promise you great rewards, those rewards are always harder to achieve than might be stated. There is an ancient saying that it might have been wise for the new chief architect to have remembered.

'Beware the deals you make with gods, for they are devious bastards, and you seldom get what you bargained for.'

Gods are quick to reward, quick to anger and like young children their rages are something to behold...but only from a safe distance.

Of the principal Gods, Aiasier is clearly the most powerful. The Lord of the sky and the vault of heaven. Within his gift is the sun and the wind and the rain. He is the god of storms.

Meura owns the waters and the seas, and she too can cast storms that ravage the land.

Ty-shour, the tangled god who sits at the roots of all things, rules the roots of the world. He rules the roots of all things in fact, including conspiracies and deceit. He can cast quakes that lay waste to continents and is the bringer of fire from the mountains.

Velvet Schem is the lady of the night. She rules the darkness and the moon and is beloved of thieves and assassins for she conceals them from prying eyes.

The Nameless God, called by many Mother Death, the carrion queen, the woman made of crows, rules over the two ends of every life. She guides souls into the world and leads them out of it and into her own realm of the dead when their lives end.

And Bera rules the creatures that crawl upon the earth and the plants and trees that grow upon it. She is the Green Queen, the Mother of Beasts, the goddess of the wild, the hunger that is never satisfied.

There were other gods, but they fell in the war that preceded the compact of the Elcardia. They no longer have power upon the earth, though the Dwarves still worship Gilliath the Maker, it is said.

You may be thinking that Bera does not appear to have any of the great power that Aiasier or Meura possess. But, it is a fact of life on Ty-Gate that it would be a grave mistake to underestimate any of the Gods.

We left the new chief architect of Avalor standing before the bronze cast doors of the temple of Ty-Shour, a god who did not much love the idea that a new and even more impressive temple to another god was to be built in a city he thought he ruled. And though Ty-Shour was deeply offended, he was also torn.

He could easily have left well alone. The construction of the temple would have failed, and the architect would have taken a short flight without the benefit of wings, and the king of Avalor would have suffered the great embarrassment and indignity of a failed vow, and the ridicule of his peers, but little else. This was not enough to pay back the slight Ty-Shour felt he had been paid. So he drew the architect in to his temple and whispered seductively in his ears of how he might complete the magnificent temple within the allotted time, if only he would promise to do all that Ty-Shour demanded.

'Now you asked a very good question.' The god said to the architect. 'Where can you build this temple? Well...I see only one place. You must build it on the green heart. Bera can hardly complain, the building is to honour the consort of the king of heaven, Aiasier will support you for he loves Velvet Schem and always wishes to see her celebrated. What's more, did Bera not give trees from her own groves to the King of Chun for the construction of his temple to Aiasier? She can hardly do less for you, now, can she.'

'But the time...' Cried the architect. 'I have so little time!'

'You forget.' Said Ty-Shour. 'I am the god of the root of all things, and the root of all buildings are their foundations. You worry about the walls and the roof and making the place look pretty. Leave the foundations to me. Trust me, I will make sure the temple is built on the foundations such a building deserves.'

Now, remembering what I have already said about the deals gods make, it is possible that the architect should have been more attentive here. But he was so grateful to Ty-Shour and so full of relief that he had a way forward, that he quite disregarded the simple fact that what he heard, and what Ty-Shour meant were very, very different things.

He agreed to the god's bargain, and hurried back to the king with the good news.

'Well, that all sounds very promising!' Said the King, 'You'd better begin!'

The King of Avalor had never met Bera, indeed, he had never

even seen her. Since she made the gift of land to his ancestor she had had little to do with the humans in the world. She tolerated them, but nothing more. Gods are very precise. When they make a deal, they stick to their part of it and, however one-sided that deal might be, they expect you to stick to your side too. But the King also knew that, despite whatever Ty-Shour might have said, you can't just chop down swathes of the Gods own domain without asking first.

It must be said that he tried.

He sent heralds into the Green Heart to call for an audience. They returned days later, hungry and tired with tales of trees that blocked their way, of paths that led back to where they started and the only answer to their calls the sound of silence and the echo of their own words.

The King set drummers on the walls and heralds called from the battlements but all they heard was the wind in the branches and the angry cawing of crows.

He set archers on the highest towers and they shot message arrows high into the air, and far across the great sea of trees, but nothing drew a response of any kind. Even the Elves were absent. Avalor had traded with the Elven Nations, but the Elves are nomadic and make no permanent settlements, they spend their lives following the seasons through the world.

Now the Architect came to the King. "My Lord. It is already spring, and two months have passed since you gave me my great task. We must start to build, or the year and a day will be up."

And so, caught between his vow and his fear of angering the Gods, the King of Avalor came to a fateful decision.

"Mark out the land you need beyond the western gate" he ordered. "Begin the felling of the trees but proclaim daily as you do so that we build to honour of the queen of heaven!"

And so, the work began. And it continued day after day for many weeks until a great open space had been carved out of the glades of the Green Heart, and piles of logs lay in heaps waiting to be used to build the frame of the new temple.

News travels fast in the woods. Birds and insects carry stories, shrews and mice gossip and brag. Foxes whisper to badgers and quiz squirrels before they munch them, and trees speak to each other. Bera had not heard any of the heralds of Avalor, why would she, they were not her people! But she heard the whispers of the massacre of groves beneath the walls of the human city, and she raged.

First, she sent the Elves. They came like a tidal wave out of the trees and killed all they caught, and once they had driven all the humans who could escape back behind the walls of their city, they burned the site of the new temple to the ground.

How did the King of Avalor respond?

Why, with fury.

How he raged. His people dead, his temple raised to the ground before it was even complete, and the day of his shame looming ever larger and ever closer.

"Burn down that forest!" he roared, and his people obeyed. High on the battlements of Avalor they raised great engines of war, catapults that could throw bales of flaming hay high over the trees to crash into the woods where they set light to everything. Soon the forest was burning and columns of black and twisting smoke went up into the heavens.

"Bright Aiasier, I send you the smoke of the forest as offering!" the King of Avalor called to the sky. Perhaps he thought that if Aiasier, the lord of light and the vault of heaven approved his plan, then Bera could not oppose it. But Aiasier did not heed him. Powerful he may be, but even Aiasier knew better than to involve himself in a battle between a god and a mortal.

Now the rage of Bera became incandescent. This mortal king was killing her trees and destroying her home. Back she sent the elves, and with them the creatures of the deep woods. The T'oak and the Burghan, the Mortaho and the Umbari. Like a storm they came and the walls of Avalor rang like a bell at their hammering. But they held, for they had been built by the Dwarves in payment for a favour done them by the founder of the city. For three days and three nights the elves and their creatures assailed the city, and the King stood on his ringing walls and laughed at the host broken upon the walls. His archers sent fiery shafts to kill the T'oak, and hails of arrows cut down the elves and finally the host retreated, and a brooding stillness fell across the land.

Inside the city the people began to whisper.

What would Bera do next?

What Bera did next was come herself.

Now, any normal man faced with a goddess girt for war, would probably bow very low and beg forgiveness for himself and for all his people.

You know, though, because I have said it, that the King of Avalor was not a normal man. He was quite besotted with his vow, and his victories over the forces Bera had sent against him only made him more confident.

One morning, as the sun rose over the smoking ruin of the green heart, one of his captains came running to the King of Avalor.

'My lord, there is a woman standing before the gate!'

'A woman?'

'Well...I think it's a woman...its difficult to tell!'

Let me describe what the king of Avalor saw when he went to the wall atop the gate, and you may understand that last comment.

Standing on the road just beyond arrow shot of the city walls was a figure. Short and stooped in stature. It wore a hooded drape of deep green which might have been cloth, or moss, or leaves, or pond weed, or the stinking pelt of some long dead monster.

It draped, that's all you need to know.

From the deapths of the shadowed hood, two bright leaf green eyes glimmered. In one lean and nut brown claw, twisted fingers like twigs gripped the trunk of a young tree as if it were a staff. The tree was in full leaf and bright fruits and nuts grew abundantly from its branches and its worm like roots tickled the earth as if they were alive, which they most likely were.

There was no doubt that this was Bera; the goddess of the wild herself.

On her hunched back there sat a bright red squirrel, easily the size of a cat, and in the air about it things buzzed and flitted. Small creatures the size of sparrows, but human in shape and winged like dragonflies.

Fairies.

Now Bera has many weapons. In the past she had even more, but some she lost and some were stolen. Her fairies, however; her fairies are her most feared, for they are terrible. The teeth of her wrath, they are called. The edge of her blade. Those of you who have heard the tale of the fall of Ipote might well be feeling that tingle of thrill across your scalp to know that Bera was about to unleash them against the king of Avalor...well...she was not.

The king of Avalor had made things personal for the goddess of the wild, and so she had come herself to face him.

With a flick of her wrist she sent the fairies away. It is not to be doubted that the people standing on the walls of the city felt some level of relief to see it, for there is very little that can stop a fairy. Perhaps, if there is time, I will tell you the story of the fall of Ipote, then you will understand.

Now. Bera seemed to do nothing. She simply stood, her bright green eyes staring at the king of Avalor as the king of Avalor stared back.

Hours passed.

The sun completed it's passage across the sky and the moon followed, and still Bera stood before the walls of the city that had been built upon the land she had gifted.

A strange siege, you may think.

It was the king who broke first.

'Bring her inside!' he snapped. 'Take her captive.'

What was he thinking? I can hear the outrage in your heads. 'He wouldn't do that!' you're thinking. 'He wouldn't bring the goddess inside his walls…that's just foolish…'

Well, haven't we already established that this king was foolish, and over proud, and…slightly deluded?

The gates creaked open and a host of armoured soldiers trotted out, weapons drawn…as if a little bit of steel and a few spears could harm a goddess…they approached Bera, who stood patiently waiting, her bright green-fire eyes glittering with fury. The squirrel on her hunch sat up and chittered and tossed nuts and berries from the top of her staff at the approaching soldiers, but they did little harm. They bounced off shields and helmets and lodged themselves between the stones of the road, or landed in the damp, sooty earth.

The soldiers surrounded Bera, and with the tips of their spears they prodded her into the city. And as she walked, with every step as her feet touched the ground, things fell from the hem of her robes. Dust and dirt and tiny little creatures. Worms and beetles and all manner of creatures were shed from her.

If anyone noticed, they gave it less thought than they should have. After all, when you are riding the back of a lion, you don't worry overmuch that it might have fleas, do you?

Now the king of Avalor was overjoyed. To his mind, you see, he had beaten the goddess of the wild. After a time of dancing a little jig of happiness at her capture, he issued three commands.

'Find my chief architect. Begin construction. We will use the greatest oaks from her most sacred grove for our temple columns...'

'Parade her throughout the city so that all my people can see how complete our victory is, then take her to the deepest, darkest and most miserable cell and lock her inside where she can never get out.'

'I want a feast. A great victory feast to celebrate our great victory, oh...this is going to be a day to remember....'

And so, Bera was paraded through the winding streets as the cheering crowds looked on, booing, hissing, and jeering as she passed. But no one seemed to notice that everywhere she went she left clouds of dust and seeds and twigs and dirt in her wake.

And then finally, Bera was taken down and down into the bowels of the earth beneath the city and locked in a tiny cell behind doors made of iron. And again, with each step she took she shed dust and twigs and dirt from her robes.

The king of Avalor retired to his castle and began to prepare for the victory feast and Bera crossed her legs and settled herself on the damp earth floor of her cell and began to sing.

And as she sang, the dust and the twigs and the dirt that had fallen from her robes. began to grow.

Out from beneath her the wave of growth spread. Flowers,

grasses, trees all reaching upwards.

Out of the cell door the wave of growth spread, up the spiraling stairs and out into the open air.

Down all the twisting route of her procession through the city, roots burrowed deep, trees swelled with obscene speed, becoming seedlings in moment, then faster than an eye could blink they were saplings, then tall and stately full grown trees, their canopies spreading to block out the sun and their roots cracking and shattering the stones of the city streets and houses.

And from each newborn tree came creatures, as if they had been born fully formed within the plants themselves. Spiders the size of hounds, bees and wasps bigger than the span of a hand, squirrels and a million, million birds until the city was alive with them.

And the people, what of them. For surely they did not just sit and watch as the forest reclaimed their city?

Well, no. Most of them tried to flee. But when they reached the gates they found that the burned and ruined wasteland beyond the city walls was once again verdant green and forested. And the road down which they would have fled was gone, broken and uprooted by oak trees that had grown suddenly from the nuts and fruits and acorns thrown by the squirrel that had accompanied Bera.

The people of Avalor found that they had nowhere to run, save a forest grown impossibly against their very walls. A dark, and brooding, and sinister place that reeked of anger and danger.

Very few were brave enough to enter it.

And the king? What was he doing as Bera's trees grew and his city crumbled to ruin? Well, he and his court feasted within the great hall of his castle as trees and vines grew about it, blocking up the windows and sealing up the doors.

And whilst those trees grew, turning the castle into a tomb, the trees that grew in Bera's cell cracked open the door and broke through the walls and ceilings, and Bera simply walked out of her prison, and out of the city and never looked back.

* * *

On the anniversary of his marriage to the princess of Avalor, the king of Chun, his wife, and their entire court traveled the kings road to Avalor to see the marvelous temple that had been built to honour the goddess of the moon. And because he was a man who wanted deeply for his father in law to love him, he had brought with him his allies, Kings Queens from half a handful of nations, so that they also could see the glorious temple the kingdom of Avalor had raised.

But, they found that crossing their path was an impenetrable wall of green. And though they sent scouts to the left and to the right of the road, they could discover no way through, and no way past and no way over it.

But the daughter of the king of Avalor was angered by the loss of her father's city, and she prevailed upon her husband to cut down the trees that blocked her way.

Now, being a man who loved his wife, he agreed. He turned to his allies and asked them for aid to cut a swathe of land clear of trees so that they could find lost Avalor. Of course, they agreed. And unwittingly brought upon Chun and Lish, and Lughannn, and Myacar the enmity of Bera and of the elves and the forest.

And that is the story of how the war between men and elves began. With a wedding and with jealousy and with pride and arrogance.

But there, you see, although we have reached the end of the

story of how Bera reclaimed her gift, stories actually never end, they just carry on in a different direction, or with different heroes or villains.

About the Author

Hi.

I just want to thank you for reaching the end of this book, and also to ask a favour.

I write because I love to write and I love to tell stories. I'd love to know what you thought of this story because, at the end of the day, if my books are not enjoyed then I'm doing something wrong.

I'm an independent writer, which means I write and publish without the support of infrastructure of a major publisher or an agent. The only parts of this process that I hand over to others are editing and cover design. Without those two skill sets, this would be a much poorer book.

If you've read this book, please leave a rating on Amazon or Goodreads to let others know how you felt about it.

Please also leave some words to tell me what you liked, or

didn't like. I would obviously love it if all the ratings were 5 stars, but in all honesty, even if you hated it know that any constructive review helps.

You can find my page on Goodreads. Search for *Michael S Evans*

Find me on Twitter @ScatteredKing

You can also find me on PATREON at *'Fantasy Books and Stories From The Nine Fold Gate'*

Also by Mike Evans

The Scattered King

Gilliath, The Maker, has been betrayed by his fellow gods. His soul was carved into nine fragments and scattered across the world. The most potent part sent through the Ninefold Gate to the realm of death. All to prevent his ever returning to unmake the world he created. But now the Ninefold Gate is broken, and Gilliath has returned and is seeking the scattered parts of his soul. And the gods who betrayed him, well, they are frightened.

Brennus, a retired soldier turned inn keeper, is unwillingly recruited by the Carrion Queen, the Goddess of Death herself, to find Gilliath and prevent his resurrection; a task made all the more perilous because Gilliath can take possession of anyone. Brennus and his friends find themselves in a desperate fight for survival, and some will fall.

Snee, former captain of the night guard of T'eag , finds her past returns to haunt her through the words of a false prophet who knows far too much about her deepest secrets. She must fight to save not only herself but her oldest friends from the vengeance of a monster she thought she had escaped long ago. And though she does not know it, one of those friends holds the secret to the location of all of the scattered parts of Gilliath's soul.

Iordanis, elf assassin to Bera, Goddess of the Wild, is sent into the human world to finish a task she failed years earlier. She finds herself fighting alongside people she has considered enemies for all her life against demons from the deepest reaches of the earth.

The Pursuit of Wolves

When the harbinger leads the wolves from the wild

and the price of the world is the life of a child...

Ravenna has returned to the Secret City to warn her people of the rebirth of Gilliath, but she does not find the welcome she expected. Danger stalks the streets of her home. A danger that she alone must fight.

In the ragged hills the town of Keller is besieged by monsters who have already left a trail of desolated towns in their wake. Caught between the monsters and his friends, Harlon, Cora and their friends must find a way to survive.

In Carcamesh, Connor begins a quest to uncover the dark conspiracy that lies at the heart of the city of mages; a conspiracy that has already embroiled his family and threatens to destroy them all.

And in Ashay, Brennus stands alone. On trial for crimes against the Emperor.

The Eye of Chaos

War is kindling.

In Pont, Brennus finds a city beset by enemies; but are the elves of the Great Green the true enemy, or are the forces of Ashay causing havoc across the land?

In T'eag, Gargrave and the forces of the secret city prepare to fight the armies of the avatar queen, but in a strange land, who can they trust?

Hunted by wolven, the few survivors of the town of Keller must find a place of safety.

Iuxime, Princess of Ashay, must find a way to stop her brother, the emperor, from destroying not only the land of Pont, but also the dwarf kingdom of Hugharan-Vash.

And across the world the gods are stirring, preparing themselves for the coming of the Lord of Chaos.

Shedding Skins: The Mages of Carcamesh Book 1

Connor is unique in all the history of magic. He is both a Mage, and a Soul Keeper; a thing never before seen. And he has made a vow. He will destroy the secret evil that sits at heart of the mage city of Carcamesh; the immortal High Mages who extend their lives through the use of terrible magics.

But the high mages are supremely powerful. To destroy them, Connor must use all of his skill and power; though even that may not be enough.

And even as he searches for a way to destroy them, the high mages are searching for him.

Along the way he discovers new friends and allies, and new enemies. And he uncovers secrets that reach back to the god war and the breaking of the world.

The Mages of Carcamesh is set within the same world, and is contemporary with The Nine Fold Gate series,

Milton Keynes UK
Ingram Content Group UK Ltd.
UKHW012220150124
436080UK00006B/478